Richard Gordon was born in 1921. He qualified as a doctor and then went on to work as an anaesthetist at St Bartholomew's Hospital, and then as a ship's surgeon. As obituary-writer for the *British Medical Journal*, he was inspired to take up writing full time and he left medical practice in 1952 to embark on his 'Doctor' series. This proved incredibly successful and was subsequently adapted into a long-running television series.

Richard Gordon has produced numerous novels and writings all characterised by his comic tone and remarkable powers of observation. His *Great Medical Mysteries* and *Great Medical Discoveries* concern the stranger aspects of the medical profession whilst his *The Private Life of...* series takes a deeper look at individual figures within their specific medical and historical setting. Although an incredibly versatile writer, he will, however, probably always be best known for his creation of the hilarious 'Doctor' series.

Doctor on the Brain

Richard Gordon

HOUSE OF
STRATUS

This edition published in 2001 by House of Stratus, an imprint of Stratus Holdings plc, 24c Old Burlington Street, London, W1X 1RL, UK.

www.houseofstratus.com

Typeset, printed and bound by House of Stratus.

A catalogue record for this book is available from the British Library.

ISBN 1-84232-507-8

1

At eight o'clock on a June morning of gauzy London sunshine, the dean of St Swithin's Hospital settled at his study desk, clicked down his ballpoint, and with an expression of intense solemnity started to write.

The tragic death yesterday of Sir Lancelot Spratt FRCS, senior surgeon at St Swithin's, leaves a gap which is only too obvious.

The dean frowned. No, that didn't seem right at all. And it wasn't every day a man found himself writing for the columns of the country's top newspaper. He stared for some time in thought through the open first-floor window of his new home, across a small walled back garden lively with blue delphiniums, pink and yellow lupins and scarlet salvias, towards the exuberantly variegated buildings of St Swithin's itself. Abruptly slashing out the lines, he started again.

The tragic death yesterday of Sir Lancelot Spratt FRCS, senior surgeon at St Swithin's, removes a highly colourful figure from not only the operating theatre but the theatre of life.

Much better! the dean decided. Quite literary, in fact. With more confidence he continued,

Sir Lancelot's rumbustious personality endeared him to many, though admittedly his close colleagues at St Swithin's sometimes found it trying. His dominating mannerisms, such as hurling surgical instruments — once, an amputated leg! — at nurses and students, were unfortunately not restricted to the operating table. He was always liable to be somewhat rough-tongued. Indeed, downright bad-tempered. One could even go so far as calling him outrageously pig-headed. Not to mention aggravatingly self-centred and quite painfully self-opinionated. Oh, yes, he had a sense of humour — or so he claimed. But it was the humour of the schoolroom, I should have said the lower fourth —

'Oh, damn!' The dean ripped the paper in two.

'*De mortuis nil nisi bonum* and all that rubbish, I suppose. Though I really don't see why a man's kicking the bucket should oblige his friends to turn themselves into a bunch of hypocrites.'

The door opened, and he was interrupted by his wife appearing with a tray.

'There you are, Lionel! I wondered where on earth you'd got to. I've brought up your second cup of coffee, as you just disappeared from breakfast like a flash.'

'I thought I'd better get on with Sir Lancelot's obituary notice straight away.'

'Oh!' She too assumed a befittingly reverent look. 'It must be an unhappy task.'

'Unhappy? It's utterly impossible! How can anyone draw a reasonably accurate pen-picture of Lancelot without seeming insulting to his memory? You might try writing a history of Jack the Ripper while delicately avoiding the subject of homicide.'

'Couldn't you concentrate on his nicer qualities?'

'I can't think of any offhand.'

'Let me see… "He was an accomplished after-dinner speaker"?'

'Rubbish. He only had one joke, and I had to hear it about five hundred times.'

' "He was a charming and generous host"?'

The dean snorted into his coffee. He was a short, gnome-like man with a pointed bald head, who sat bouncing gently in his chair – his habit during the flashes of exasperation from the explosive little storms which blew so regularly through his life.

'Why, it was only last month he gave that delightful party for the students' union ball, which we all enjoyed so much,' the dean's wife said.

'*I* didn't enjoy it. I happen particularly to dislike the students' union ball. They all become far too familiar and expect me to pay for their drinks. I should have avoided it altogether this year, had Muriel not been president of the union.'

'It really is awfully difficult to think of Lancelot as "the late". All our married life I've always regarded him as completely indestructible, like the Himalayas.'

The dean gave a sigh. 'It comes to us all, I suppose, Josephine. However much one tries to suppress it, this sort of task does give one a distinctly chilly feeling up and down the spine.'

'But it's Lancelot's obituary, dear, not your own.'

'Nevertheless, it brings home rather forcefully that all men are mortal and medical science is on occasion inclined to be somewhat unreliable.' He fluttered a hand. ' "Never send to know for whom the bell tolls; it tolls for thee... The paths of glory lead but to the grave... *Ars longa, vita brevis...*" All that sort of thing, you know.'

'But Lionel, darling!' Josephine was a tall, good-looking, dark-haired, kind-hearted woman, whose soft grey eyes now filmed over with compassion. 'You're still a comparatively young man.'

'I'm a deal older than you.' The dean took off his large round glasses and polished them vigorously. 'You were really so young when we married, Josephine – in those days, quite a child-bride. Now of course girls seem to start raising families between sitting their O-level papers. I suppose it's because they get more meat in their diet, or something.'

Standing behind his chair, she looped her arms gently across his shoulders. 'Promise me you won't entertain any more of those gloomy thoughts?'

'But it's difficult, my dear. I must admit, that for some time now I've had feelings of...well, the utter pointlessness of life. Its complete futility. Surely you must have noticed something about me?'

'I put it down to your old rheumatism playing up.'

'Why are we here? What is our use? From the neonatal cry to the death-rattle?'

'Lionel – !'

'We are but leaves which fall in autumn, to be tidied up and turned into smoke drifting hopefully in the direction of Heaven.'

'Lionel! You're upsetting me.'

'Life goes on like an alarm-clock. Tick-tock, tick-tock, tick-tock...then suddenly dingalingalingalingaling.'

'Lionel! This lovely morning, too.' He leant back on the comforting elasticity of her substantial bosom. 'But quite apart from being a physician, and doing so much good for people, you've led such a successful life.'

'Perhaps that's the trouble? By middle-age I've achieved my ambitions. Every single one. That's the Devil's own punishment for an able man.'

'Aren't you proud of your new knighthood?'

'It only opens another hole in your pocket,' he said churlishly. 'Everyone seems to imagine that because you've got a title you're rolling in it. Anyway, there suddenly seem to be knights everywhere, as thick on the ground as traffic wardens. I remember it was just the same when I qualified. The entire world suddenly seemed populated exclusively with doctors. Odd. Anyway, this came in the morning post. It might possibly provide me with some fresh interest in life.'

He reached for a letter on crested House of Commons paper. Josephine read it over his shoulder.

Dear Lionel,

Can I possibly buy you lunch one day very soon? Today, if you like. A matter of great importance and urgency has arisen in one of my committees. I think you might very well be interested.

As ever,
Frankie.

'That sounds promising, dear. Perhaps the chairmanship of a royal commission?'

'Knowing Frankie, more like the chairmanship of a local political garden party. But I'll get my secretary to phone.' He dropped the letter back on his desk. 'It's always fun to see old Frankie again.'

His wife removed her arms, he thought a shade abruptly. 'If you ask me, you're only getting these quite unjustified feelings of uselessness because our two children have grown up and are leaving home.'

'Ah! A delightful feminine over-simplification. Though I must say it's strange to think of young George as married, and living in Sweden – and God knows what the pair of them are getting up to, judging by the Swedish film posters plastered all over London. And now Muriel's almost a qualified doctor…'

The dean's eye softened as it fell on their elder child's photograph beside the pad of lined foolscap on his desk. His daughter Muriel took after her mother, but the dark hair was drawn back severely to display an intellectual brow, the full lips, which could look as inviting as fresh strawberries, were set in an austere line, and the soft, dreamy eyes seemed to be studying some fascinating rash on the nose of the photographer. 'I suppose we must be grateful she's turned out such a level-headed, serious-minded girl. Not like some of these sex-mad flibbertigibbets you find among the female students these days – even in St Swithin's, I'm ashamed to say. I do so hope she wins the gold medal in clinical medicine.' His tone was heartfelt. 'It's just bad luck she's got such opposition this year. Young Sharpewhistle, you know. The man's perfectly abnormal. An intellectual freak. His brains quite frighten me, sometimes, in the wards.' The dean busily clicked his ballpoint several times. 'Well, my dear, I must get on. Before I go to the hospital I must get Sir Lancelot sewn up, as it were. What are you doing this morning?'

'Monday's my day for physiotherapy.'

'I was forgetting. I hope that girl in St Swithin's is doing you good? Thank heavens I never let Lancelot succeed in looking at that back of yours! He'd have had a dirty great slit down it in no time at all. Absolute sadists, these surgeons. I suppose that's what drives them to take up such an abnormal occupation at all.'

Once alone, the dean warmed to his task. With the help of *Who's Who* and the *Medical Directory* he rapidly covered four of the foolscap pages, which he read through with a satisfaction approaching smugness. It really was awfully good, he decided. And who knows? he wondered, slipping the paper into an envelope. The editor might be sufficiently impressed to invite him to contribute future articles on a somewhat less specialized topic. For a substantial fee, of course. Envelope in hand, the dean hurried downstairs. He collected his hat and briefcase in the narrow hallway. He called a goodbye to his wife. He opened his front door and stepped into the morning sunshine.

The front door led down a short flight of steps directly on to the pavement. The dean lived in No 2 Lazar Row, the middle of three newly-built joined together three-storey houses which occupied a short cul-de-sac against the walls of the hospital itself. To his left as he emerged, the door of No 3 was ajar. Its householder stood on the front step, a bundle of letters in his hand, sniffing the air while gathering his morning post. He was almost fully dressed, with formal striped trousers, a white shirt and a St Swithin's tie, though wearing instead of a jacket a scarlet silk dressing-gown decorated with large, fearsome golden dragons.

'Morning, Lancelot,' called the dean cheerfully. 'Charming day.'

Sir Lancelot Spratt grunted.

'I'll be seeing you in the hospital at lunch?'

'Doubtless.'

The dean braced his shoulders. 'I must say, I feel I've done one good day's work already. A splendid feeling to start the week. Eh?'

'I should myself much prefer to be spending the morning watching cricket at Lord's.'

'Then why not?' urged the dean. 'Why not play truant? We must snatch our pleasures while we can. Who knows? You may be taken from us this very afternoon.'

'That eventuality was not foremost in my plans for the day.'

'Well, I must be off. There's always a lot of medical school business to get through before my ward round. So convenient, isn't it, being able to stroll from one's home to one's work? I honestly don't know how I put up with that dreadful West End traffic for so long, when we lived near Harley Street. Quite the shrewdest thing I ever did in my life, moving here next door to you.' Sir Lancelot glared. The dean tipped up his chin and took a deep breath. The warm sunshine and the knowledge of the paper in his pocket had momentarily melted his inner gloom. 'A morning like this, Lancelot – doesn't it make you feel glad that you're alive?'

'I have no idea how I should feel were I experiencing the alternative.'

'I mean, doesn't it fill you with *joie de vivre*? Make you think life's worth living? After all, our time is short –'

Sir Lancelot had shut the door.

The dean hurried away with a thoughtful frown. Really, the fellow's becoming surlier than ever, he decided. He had known Sir Lancelot since he had himself been a house physician and Sir Lancelot the St Swithin's resident surgical officer. He had long ago discovered – or as the dean would himself have put it, had bitterly suffered – all the surgeon's idiosyncrasies. But over the past four weeks, since about the time of the students' union May ball, a distinct change for the worse had come over his neighbour. He had seemed more withdrawn, the dean felt. Preoccupied with something. Nervous, ready to jump at a sudden sound, quite unlike his usual unshakable self.

He remembered how Sir Lancelot's eye, when you were talking to him, sometimes wandered as though searching for someone who wasn't there. Very sinister. Once the dean had overheard him talking to himself in his garden, extremely loudly. Premature senility, the dean thought sombrely. Softening of the brain. After all those years of self-indulgence, Sir Lancelot's arteries must be so hardened it was a wonder he didn't crackle when he moved. The dean's bouncy step turned through the hospital gates into the main courtyard. It was sad, but…well, he had been prudent, writing that obituary the very morning the editor's letter requesting it had arrived.

Sir Lancelot too had a first-floor study overlooking the walled rear garden, which had a tiny close-cropped lawn, orderly pink and white rose bushes, and variously coloured stocks arranged as neatly as chocolates in a box. He stood in the middle of the study floor, still in his dressing-gown, reading the first of his letters through half-moon glasses. He slowly stroked his beard for some moments in thought. He raised his thick gingery eyebrows. He reached his decision. With a sigh he sat at his desk, which was separated from the dean's by only a few inches of brickwork.

'I suppose one has one's duty. Even if it is sometimes a depressing and possibly a painful one.' Sir Lancelot uncapped his fountain-pen and reached for a pad of lined foolscap. 'Might as well get on with it here and now, I suppose.'

In bold, flowing hand Sir Lancelot began,

The tragic death yesterday of Sir Lionel Lychfield FRCP, dean of St Swithin's, was an event of more importance to his small circle of friends than to the world at large.

Sir Lancelot grunted. No, that wouldn't do. He crossed out the words and tried again.

The tragic death yesterday of Sir Lionel Lychfield FRCP, dean of St Swithin's, will grieve the many who admired him only through reputation even more than the few privileged to know him personally.

His pen scratched on powerfully. He had always felt a talent for that sort of prose.

2

The main courtyard of St Swithin's Hospital was separated from a busy north London shopping street of stereotyped ugliness by a line of tall, stout, spiked iron railings, from which the students occasionally suspended banners announcing rag week or their objection to aspects of the political situation, or unpopular members of their own fraternity by their trousers. Inside were half a dozen venerable plane-trees and a pair of statues in memory of the hospital's distinguished Victorian sons – Lord Larrymore, a physician like the dean, who claimed to have discovered the cause of tuberculosis had he not been forestalled by a bunch of damn foreigners like Robert Koch. And Sir Benjamin Bone, a surgeon like Sir Lancelot Spratt, who would have been appointed to Her Majesty's household had the Queen not found his bluff, jolly bedside manner not at all amusing.

The ascetic-looking Lord Larrymore sat in academic robes with an expression of querulousness, left hand forever extended, as though arguing some arcane clinical point across the courtyard with Sir Benjamin. They had not in fact spoken during the final twenty years of their lives, following some complicated quarrel of which they and everyone else had forgotten the cause, communicating with bleakly polite notes transmitted by a hospital porter employed expressly for the purpose. Sir Benjamin stood in full-skirted frock-coat, a cocked head and quizzical expression as he eyed the skull in his huge hand suggesting an aging Hamlet with difficulty in hearing the prompter. Few of the busy hospital passers-by spared them a glance or a thought. Only the London pigeons continued to give them generous attention.

Even the patch of sickly-looking grass between them had now gone, cars and ambulances jamming the broad arena where once consultants clattered over the cobbles behind livened coachmen in their broughams and victorias, and their patients arrived less obtrusively, borne by the neighbours on a window-shutter. The dean hurried up the flight of stone steps to the plate-glass front doors leading to the main hall, briefly nodded good-morning to Harry the porter in his glass box, then made briskly towards his office along the wide, rubber-floored main corridor. Day and night this was always busy with hospital staff, patients on stretchers and wheelchairs, cylinders of oxygen, containers of food, trollies carrying everything from bottles of blood to the morning papers, and emitting a faint, ineradicable smell of phenol and distant long-stewing greens, to old St Swithin's men as hauntingly nostalgic as the perfume of some lost, first love.

At that moment the dean's daughter Muriel was sitting just some fifty yards away in the medical school library. She looked at her large wristwatch with its sweep second hand for the twenty-second time that morning. She bit her lip, suppressing her impatience. The moment was not yet ripe. She must control herself. Otherwise, she couldn't effectively put the carefully thought-out plan into operation.

During her final year as a medical student, Muriel generally left home in the morning before her father. She liked to hang about the casualty department, or nose round the wards – the patients conveniently being roused and exposed to medical attention since well before six a.m. – in the hope of coming upon instructive cases before the other students began crowding about. Sometimes she disappeared to the library, the gift of a Victorian brewer, with its riotously carved pale oak, vaulted ceilings and almost opaque leaded windows, then thought the necessary background to piety, justice, learning or the medical treatment of paupers. She sat in a bay lined with books, at a table with piled bound volumes of the *British Medical Journal* and *Lancet,* propped open in front of her *Recent Advances in Medicine*, at its side a note-book. That morning she had neither made a note nor read a word. She stared at the printed page through large round metal-rimmed glasses, like the dean's, as unseeing as a nervous patient behind a waiting-room magazine.

9

Muriel looked at her watch again. Two minutes and a half to nine o'clock. She stood up abruptly. Zero hour. If her timing was correct, running over the ground the morning before, she should arrive at her target precisely at the opportune moment.

She shut the volume of *Recent Advances*. She looked round anxiously. She was still alone. It was early for even a conscientious student to be found in the library, but some girl from her own year might easily have looked in to check some facts, then casually attached herself as Muriel left, ruining the whole scheme. She took off her reading-glasses and slipped them with her notebook into a capacious brown handbag. For a second her fingertips stayed in the depths. It was still there, of course. She fancied it was still even warm.

With a brisk step, Muriel turned towards the library door. She was tall, like her mother, her feet in flat shoes rather too large. Her plain brown dress was new, but like all her clothes seemed to belong to the fashion before last. Her hair was gathered into an untidy ponytail by a twisted rubber band. She was slim – when inspecting herself in her bedroom mirror on the top floor of the dean's house, as she had so frequently over the past few weeks, she had to agree that her anatomy, though no different from any other girl's, was tastefully distributed. It was a conclusion which frightened her a little. Had she tried, she could have made herself look as inviting as any of the hundreds of young women working at St Swithin's. But she told her mother she hadn't the time, and her father agreed beautification was quite unnecessary, the male students at St Swithin's being as undiscriminating as a bunch of sex maniacs newly liberated from Broadmoor.

Muriel left the library for the courtyard, but turned away from the steps of the main hospital entrance. St Swithin's had grown as haphazardly as London itself, and in the four hundred years of its existence had thrown up buildings which met in awkward corners and narrow passages all over its irregular site. She followed a flagstoned alleyway beside the Georgian maternity department, skirted the brand-new sixteen-floor steel-and-glass surgical block and with a quick glance over her shoulder made towards the red-brick baronial battlements housing the pathology laboratories. She hurried past the gothic front door, and with another apprehensive glance turned round the back, then briskly mounted the black metal fire-escape. The door leading into the third floor was slightly ajar. She had left it so the previous afternoon.

Muriel glanced right and left. The dim, bleak, green-painted passage was empty. She walked to a frosted-glass door at the end, marked in red CLINICAL PATHOLOGY. She tapped.

'Come in.'

She opened it. Mr Winterflood, pipe clamped between his teeth, tartan scarf round his neck, was just taking off his fawn raincoat. Her timing had been superb, Muriel thought. As efficient as everything else she did – well, almost everything else, she supposed, in the circumstances.

'Well! It's Miss Lychfield. And how's the dean keeping?'

'He seems very well, thank you, Mr Winterflood. I'm sorry to catch you just as you've arrived.'

'Wait a sec. I'll get my white coat on.' He unwound the scarf. 'Got to wrap up well, you know. Some of these bright mornings are treacherous. I mean, for a man with all my complaints. "A walking pathological museum", the dean once called me. Though I expect he can hardly wait to get me downstairs on the post-mortem table. Eh?'

He gave a laugh, and taking a match from the pocket of his thick woollen khaki cardigan filled the small, untidy laboratory with smoke. The chief technician was a small fat man with a thick insanitary-looking moustache and abnormally bright red cheeks. He had been a patient of St Swithin's since childhood, and if he had succeeded in rising from the severely-drilled ranks in the wards to the hospital staff itself, this was less through his abilities than his doctors' concern to keep track of him until they could discover exactly what the devil had been going on in his inside.

'I've got a specimen.' Muriel opened her bag as he pulled on his white coat. 'I thought I'd bring it up myself.'

'From one of your patients, is it?'

'Well, yes. Or rather, well, no. That is, it's from a friend.' She produced from her bag a small screw-capped hospital specimen bottle filled with straw-coloured fluid.

'What's it for?' Mr Winterflood held the bottle to the light with a knowing eye. 'Sugar and albumen?'

'Well, er, no. Pregnancy.'

'Ah.' He put the bottle with a flourish on the laboratory workbench. 'That simple little specimen, it's like a bomb, isn't it? Could change the shape of two people's lives overnight. I'm a philosophical chap. I often think about that. Some of the ladies, they go into tears of joy knowing that they're at last going to have a little one. Others…a terrible state they get into. Threaten suicide maybe. Do it sometimes, for all I know. Not so much these days, of course, when such matters can be rectified through the proper channels. But it still puts a fair cat among the pigeons. Strange, isn't it? Same event, different reaction. As I always say about this life, it's not what happens to you, it's the way you look at it. Now, if the Prime Minister took my advice—'

'When will you have the result?'

'This evening do you?'

'I'll come up.'

'Don't bother, Miss. I'll phone your friend.'

'She's not on the telephone.'

'Oh. Married, is she?'

'No.'

'Ah. I see. Might be awkward, leaving a message. She thinks she's in the pudding club, then?'

'Yes.'

'Far gone?'

'Not very. In fact, she's not *really* sure. That's why she sent the specimen.'

'Nothing like it for making a girl proper impatient, eh?' He lit his pipe again.

'That's right.'

'What's the naughty little lady's name?'

'Smith.'

'Come on!'

'Must you really have her name? She's a…very old friend.'

'I must, Miss. Lab regulations. All specimens must be clearly labelled with the patient's name, age and ward. What would happen if the professor came in and found the bottle? Could get me in the cart good and proper. Or he might easily decide to do this very test himself, to demonstrate to the students. He'd have to read out the patient's name –'

Already tense with the anxieties of the morning, Muriel felt her head swim. 'Mr Winterflood, I particularly want *you* to do that test. The professor mustn't come near it. You see, it's mine.'

'Oh.' Mr Winterflood picked up the bottle again and inspected it with more reverence.

'*Please* will you do this for me?' Muriel implored. 'Of course, it may well be negative. But even so, I don't want the news of it to get about the hospital. Surely you can see that?'

'Don't worry, Miss. You can rely on my professional discretion. I'll mark your name on it in pencil, and rub it out immediately afterwards. How's that?'

Muriel looked nervously at her watch. She had chosen her moment carefully, before the professor usually arrived. But he could walk in any time, and he was an old friend of her father's who had punctured her as a baby with her immunizing injections. It was essential he knew nothing of it. 'That sounds a very sensible arrangement, Mr Winterflood. I must run along now, but I'll be back at five-thirty.'

'Right you are. Let's hope it's just a false alarm, eh?'

Muriel hurried down the fire-escape and retraced her path to the courtyard. She still had twenty minutes before appearing in the wards for her father's teaching round. She had been allotted an interesting case of thyrotoxicosis, and particularly wanted to shine as she presented it to the class. But it was difficult to think adequately about work, or about anything, with that little bottle in Mr Winterflood's laboratory deciding the shape of her entire life to come. As she mounted the stone steps, a voice called her name.

Muriel spun round. 'Tulip? Where had you got to? I haven't seen you since the night of the union ball.

'Oh, I had my midder to finish, then I went to Torremolinos for a fortnight.'

'But how super. Have a good time?'

'Oh, great. All those dreamy pink Scandinavians working off a lifetime's inhibitions as their epidermis peeled in the sun.'

The two girls pushed open the plate-glass doors. Tulip Twyson was neither shapelier nor better looking than Muriel, but her skill in making the most of basic ingredients was like an experienced French chef against a suburban housewife. Her long blonde hair hung loose, her rather sharp face was fashionably tanned, and she wore skirts so short that the dean was continually mystified at the rate the male members of his bedside classes managed to drop their pencils.

'Tulip,' asked Muriel. 'Will you do me a tremendous favour? If anyone asks, say I spent the night after the May ball in your flat.'

Tulip raised her eyebrows. 'No problem. But who was it?'

'I'd rather not say.'

'OK. What was he like as a performer?'

'Oh…well…I wouldn't know.'

'You mean, you'd passed out?'

'No, not at all. But you see, Tulip…and this is something I'd only tell *you*… I'd never done it before. Ever.'

'Virtuous you.'

'I've never seemed to have the time.' She looked apologetic. 'All my life, I've devoted myself to my work. That's partly through Father, I suppose. You know how severe he is. He thinks I ought to qualify – even win the gold medal – before I start thinking about men.'

'He's like those schoolmistresses who told you masturbation ruins your hockey. Personally, I always found it less exhausting and very much warmer.'

'I know I'm an adult. Why, I'm almost middle-aged compared with some girls I've known who've got married. But I've a career to make. I'm determined on that, you know. I'd really love to be the first female consultant ever elected to the St Swithin's staff.'

'We all have our strange ambitions, love.'

'After all, my father is the dean, and he'd help. That sort of thing goes on all the time at St Swithin's. But he certainly wouldn't if he thought I'd let him down.'

'A pity nothing came of your thing with lovely little Terry Summerbee.'

'That was the trouble. He was a bit too lovely. Other girls got their claws into him while I was toiling over my books.'

14

They walked along the main corridor for a moment in silence.

'Tulip –' Muriel burst out. 'Tulip, I'm very worried.'

'Oh, you'll win that gold medal, I'm sure.'

'I'm worried that something went wrong. After the ball.'

Tulip stopped. 'Are you overdue?'

'Just about.'

'But didn't you take precautions?'

'Of course. Or rather, he did. In fact, he took two. One on top of the other.'

'H'm…those things can let you down, you know. They say there's a twenty per cent failure rate, though God knows how the statisticians get the figures. Crawl round pub car parks on Saturday nights, I suppose. But aren't you on the pill, and safe for good and all?'

'You don't always carry an umbrella if you live in the desert.'

'No, I suppose not. Well, pregnancy is an eminently curable condition these days.'

'But think of the complications! My father –'

'He needn't know.'

'He will.'

'Well, that's your problem, I suppose.' Tulip was running out of sympathy. 'After the union ball, eh? I must say, you seem to have taken your duties as president rather too seriously.'

'I'd never have done what I did, I'm sure, except I'd been drinking a lot of champagne with our party. And I did in fact ask the advice of someone very mature and experienced.'

'What did she say?' Tulip was curious.

'It wasn't a she. It was…another doctor. He said to go ahead and enjoy it. Otherwise, when I did qualify I'd be so busy catching up lost time I'd make Fanny Hill look like Florence Nightingale.' Muriel stopped dead. Immediately ahead, approaching down the corridor, was her mother. Muriel's brain was so strained that morning, she imagined confusedly that her secret trip to Mr Winterflood had already somehow leaked out to the dean. 'I only went up to check on a blood-sugar,' she said at once.

'What's that, dear? Hello, Tulip, you look as though you've been lying under a hot sun somewhere.'

'What are you doing here?' Muriel demanded.

'I'm only a patient,' her mother replied mildly. 'I've come for my physiotherapy. But are you all right, dear? You look as though you'd just remembered you'd left a cupboardful of instruments inside a patient.'

'I…I was thinking. About Daddy's teaching round.'

'Oh, yes, it's almost time, isn't it? And by the way, when he shows you a young man in the corner with puzzling neuritis, the real diagnosis is acute porphyria. He was talking about it in his sleep.'

Muriel and Tulip went on towards the wards. But Muriel had one more task yet that trying morning. Making some excuse, she doubled back towards the students' common-room. There were a handful of male students there, standing admiringly round Edgar Sharpewhistle.

The young man's intellectual fame had by then spread far beyond St Swithin's. As a contestant in the television show *IQ Quiz* he could display his massive brain-power at peak viewing time every Thursday night to some ten million rapt if mystified spectators. Never a man slavishly to court popularity, Sharpewhistle was gratified at the interest shown in him by his fellows, and their new solicitude for his bodily health and mental tranquillity. He felt he had been perfectly right in imagining, since his arrival at St Swithin's as a junior student, that his personal qualities had been overlooked by his contemporaries, often deliberately.

'The last question was really very simple,' he was explaining. 'The old odd-word game. You pick the odd word out of five. The answer, you might remember, was "Loathsome". It was just a matter of noticing that the number of letters between the first and last of each word was three times that of the letters in the word plus three. See? "Loathsome" didn't fit into the series. No trouble, really. Took me eighteen seconds by the clock.'

'And you're through to the next round?' asked a tall, elegant student called Roger Duckham.

'That's it. Mind you, it gets tougher as it goes along.'

'What do you think your chances are of actually picking up the final prize, Edgar?'

'You mean the thousand quid, specially selected library and a trip for two to the Bahamas—'

'Plus a year's supply of some ghastly minced fish instant dinners, I believe?'

'Well, yes,' said Sharpewhistle shamefacedly.

'That's from the firm behind it really. Fish for brains, and those old wives' tales, you know. A pretty good chance, I'd have thought.'

'You mean, you honestly don't know the questions in advance? Not even a hint? Nothing faked at all?' Sharpewhistle looked indignant. 'Well, I hope you win it, Edgar. Very much indeed. I'm sure we all do. Don't we?'

The others agreed warmly. Sharpewhistle was unable to hide a look of pleasure, Roger Duckham having taken pains to be exquisitely arrogant towards him for years. 'I'm only doing it all for the honour of St Swithin's, of course.'

'Of course,' Roger agreed. 'Particularly as we got trounced in the rugger cup. No one who knows you, Edgar, would ever believe you wanted anything out of it yourself. Not even the fish dinners. You keep at it for the sake of us all.' He had noticed Muriel sidle into the room, and smiled at her. Everyone knew of the bitter, sometimes only faintly masked rivalry between her and Sharpewhistle over the examination for the gold medal.

'Time to go and look round before the dean's class.' Sharpewhistle picked his short white coat from a row of hooks on the wall. The brainiest student at St Swithin's was, like such other exceptionally intelligent men as Voltaire or Dr Johnston, not of a handsome presence. He was short, almost a midget, with a flat head, sandy hair drawn forward into a quiff, and a pale moustache which drooped dispiritedly over the corners of his mouth. His complexion was pink and shining, as though he had just been lifted from a pan of boiling water. His voice was squeaky and he had an armpit problem. He was dressed in plain grey trousers and a dark blue blazer with a St Swithin's crest, a throat-torch and three ballpoints in different colours arranged neatly in the pocket.

'Got your thyroid all lined up, then?' Sharpewhistle asked Muriel.

'Yes, I hope so.'

'Good. I'd like to have a quick feel of it before the round, if I may.'

'Of course.' Muriel looked quickly behind. She dropped her voice. 'I've taken the specimen up.'

'When'll you hear?'

'Half past five.'

'We'll have to wait, then, won't we?' Answering IQ questions on television had given him an admirable calmness in emergency.

3

As the dean arrived breathless outside his wards after trotting up four flights of stairs – he thought the exercise beneficial to the coronary arteries – Sir Lancelot was still in his study coming to the end of his literary exercise.

He is survived by his wife, Josephine, he wrote, *a lady of charm, tact, wide intellect, grace, good taste and generosity, whose qualities so felicitously counter-balanced his own. There are two children, one of whom follows him in the profession.*

Sir Lancelot turned back the four pages and read them closely, fountain-pen poised. But apart from a comma or two, there was really no need for alteration. He congratulated himself on so stylish a depiction of the dean's personal qualities. He supposed these had been rubbed in his face hard enough, since they had first shared cold, late meals and midnight cups of coffee as overworked residents at St Swithin's.

Sir Lancelot suddenly looked up. He straightened himself, as his body froze. His eyebrows quivered. His mouth opened. His eyes flicked anxiously from side to side. The pen started to shake violently in his hand.

'Pull yourself together…!' he muttered.

He managed to set down the pen, sitting for a moment with head in hands. With an effort, he slowly turned round in the chair, his expression indicating barely-suppressed horror at what he might see.

The study was empty.

Sir Lancelot forced himself to his feet. He squared his shoulders. With a determined stride, he looked behind a tall, wooden roll-fronted filing cabinet. Nothing. He pushed aside the single easy chair beneath the reading-lamp. An empty space. There was no more furniture in the small room, but he gingerly reached out to feel behind the curtains. No. He was alone.

'Imagination, I suppose.' He took out a red-and-white handkerchief to mop his broad forehead. 'Still, it gave me a most unpleasant turn...' His large frame shuddered. 'It must be the effect of the chronic strain these last four weeks, getting me down.' He glanced at the bracket clock in the corner, startled to see the time already past ten. He had been carried away by his literary task, and the harrowing appointment of the morning was now pressing. 'Better get going,' he went on to himself. 'Can't funk it, I suppose. Though it takes it out of a man, suffering so many weird new experiences at my age.'

Sir Lancelot slipped the dean's obituary into a desk drawer. He had thought of posting it to the editor straight away, but felt some improvements might occur to him, some little flourishes which might raise it to a classical example of its art-form. He crossed the landing to his dressing-room, changing the golden dragons for a formal black jacket. He walked sedately downstairs to face the blue-overall-covered backside of Miss Fiona MacNish, his much cherished housekeeper, who was polishing the hall floor.

'I shall be dining at home tonight.'

The housekeeper straightened up. She was a freckle-faced, sandy-haired Aberdonian, whose frank green eyes and open smile suggested white heather, buttered scones, teetotal Sundays and similar exemplary, wholesome items from north of the border. 'I thought you might like some tripe and onions.'

Sir Lancelot nodded. His favourite dish.

'And if you're in for tea, I was going to make some fresh hot buttered baps.'

'I shall, alas, be kept at the hospital this afternoon. I am taking the morning off.'

'A morning off? That's most unusual for you, Sir Lancelot, isn't it – ?' She stopped. His eyes had started to roll and his shoulders to twitch. 'Are you all right, Sir Lancelot?' she asked with deep concern.

'It's nothing, nothing...' He stared anxiously round the small hallway.

He produced the handkerchief again to mop his face. 'A spasm. Lot of it about this time of the year.'

'You haven't been yourself at all, you know. Not for weeks now. Not since that lovely champagne party you gave for the students' ball. I've been really worried about you, I don't mind admitting. I think you ought to go and see a doctor.'

'Oh, I've no faith in the medical profession. It's a touch of migraine, perhaps. Nothing to worry about.' He picked up his black homburg. 'Should anyone telephone, I am spending the morning conducting family business with my solicitors in the City.'

'Very good, Sir Lancelot.'

The surgeon stepped outside. Well, he thought, at least it's a pleasant day. Almost makes one forget the dreadful humiliation. He started to walk along the cul-de-sac, extremely slowly.

St Swithin's Hospital owned Lazar Row, the site of its sixteenth-century lazar house, where the lepers were segregated and allowed abroad only with bells or clappers to keep terrified uninfected fellow citizens at bay. When leprosy disappeared from Europe a hundred years later, the building was made over to smallpox sufferers, visited by fashionable physicians in buckskin breeches and gilt-buttoned satin coats, wigs and three-cornered hats, and gold-headed canes from which they anxiously inhaled aromatic and hopefully disinfectant herbs concealed therein. After Edward Jenner and his Gloucestershire dairymaids the lazar house fell empty, and becoming dilapidated was used for rabies sufferers and other violent lunatics, on the workmanlike theory that they would be totally unaware of their surroundings anyway. In late Victorian days, it was, like most of St Swithin's, rebuilt in the bright red brick which served with such cheerful adaptability for colleges, chapels or railway-stations, to become the isolation wards – the 'Fever Hospital', a piece of standing scenery in the nightmares of local children, to whom the stoutly-porticoed front door served only too often as the jaws of Moloch.

When antibiotics began to tame infections after the Second World War the building was turned over to the accommodation of junior nurses, and becoming too tumbledown even for this purpose was demolished. The residential area round St Swithin's, having become déclassé, was now réchauffé, with its experimental theatre, amusing little restaurants and boutiques instead of shops. A little guiltily, the hospital built the three comfortable houses on the bones of its lazars, with the excuse that the complexities of modern medicine required a senior consultant always near at hand. They were taken up eagerly, the rent being hardly more than peppercorns.

Each house had its top floor as a self-contained flat, Muriel occupying the one in the dean's home and Miss MacNish that in Sir Lancelot's. The surgeon made a point of showing his professional visitors the stout front door at the top of his staircase, Miss MacNish being comely, himself a widower, and doctors through long experience of mankind having incorrigibly dirty minds. From the top-floor flat of No 1, the house nearest the main road, a pair of large, well made-up blue eyes were at that moment watching Sir Lancelot closely as he ambled along the pavement.

'Well – !' breathed the owner of the eyes. 'And what does the old fool expect everyone to imagine he's up to?'

It was a morning of mysterious movement for the inhabitants of Lazar Row. Sir Lancelot stopped at the corner. He took out his half-hunter, put it back, clasped his hands behind his back, and stared at the sky as if weighing the chances of rain. He edged a glance over his shoulder. The row was empty. He abruptly strode towards the front door of No 1, taking off his hat and holding it in front of his face.

The woman with the blue eyes had already reached the foot of the staircase as he rang the bell.

'Good morning, Sir Lancelot.'

'Not late, I hope?' He pushed his way hastily inside, shutting the door behind him.

'It's ten-fifteen exactly.' She awarded his punctuality with a smile. She was tall, slim and fair-skinned, her blonde hair clearly tended at great expense, her make-up indicating a good deal of early morning labour, her dress simple but in the latest style. Sir Lancelot put her in the late twenties. He thought of her as the icily efficient type of modern secretary, the sort who bestowed even amiability with the measured care of a physician prescribing drugs. At that moment the lively opening bars of Mozart's *Eine Kleine Nacht Musik* came on the violin from immediately upstairs.

'I suppose he *is* expecting me, Mrs Tennant?' asked Sir Lancelot anxiously.

'Of course.' She looked reproachful. 'He has been feeling a little disturbed this morning.' Sir Lancelot followed her to the first floor. The music stopped in mid-bar as she announced, 'Dr Bonaccord, Sir Lancelot is here.'

Dr Bonaccord stood up, one hand outstretched, violin and bow in the other. 'A great pleasure, my dear fellow. We don't see nearly enough of each other. I don't think I've ever thanked you properly for that delightful champagne party, which my secretary and I enjoyed so much. It's the very first time you've set foot in this house, I believe? We really are a most unneighbourly lot in Lazar Row. Gisela, do take my violin and put it away, there's a good girl.'

'I was unaware that you were a talented amateur musician.'

'Alas, I am a very indifferent one. But I find it soothing whenever I'm in danger of developing a bad temper. "What passion cannot music raise and quell", eh? Do sit down.'

Dr Bonaccord was chubby, with pale eyes and light chestnut hair fashionably cut. He was in his early thirties. He wore an expensive dark suit which Sir Lancelot thought more suitable for a luminary of the acting profession than the medical one, with a brightly-patterned shirt and a flashy tie. He had severe-looking rimless glasses under a bulging forehead, and his face had a pinkish tinge to it. Sir Lancelot always thought of him as a highly intellectual strawberry blancmange.

Like the dean's and Sir Lancelot's studies, the room was small and overlooked a garden, which was largely filled with a hothouse containing orchids and rare pinguicula plants from South America reputed to eat flies. The walls were a cheerful primrose, the carpet and curtains mossy green, the furniture Sir Lancelot dismissed vaguely as 'Scandinavian'. In one corner was a small white statue which struck him as a boiled egg suspended by spaghetti, in another a crystal vase crammed with crimson, budding roses.

The door shut behind the secretary. Sir Lancelot continued to stare round. 'No couch?'

'I've dispensed with that prop of the comic cartoons. You'll be perfectly comfortable in the easy chair. You can put your feet up on the little pouffe.'

Sir Lancelot sat down obediently, folding his hands across his expansive stomach. He was almost horizontal, facing across the room with only the top of his head visible to Dr Bonaccord. Well, the moment has finally arrived, the surgeon thought. In a way, it was a relief. Though he still thought psychiatry the last refuge of the incompetent doctor, and Bonaccord himself as further round the bend than an acrobat's umbilicus. But desperate illnesses needed desperate remedies.

'You will not, of course, breathe a word to our colleagues at St Swithin's that I have consulted you today?'

'Naturally, I preserve professional discretion about all my patients.' Dr Bonaccord sounded hurt. 'Though I am at a loss, if I might say so, why people should hide the fact they have seen a psychiatrist. If you break a leg, you go openly enough to an orthopaedic surgeon to have it set.' He leant back, pudgy fingertips together. 'Now, I want you to forget I am here. To forget me completely. Imagine you are quite alone, addressing these four bare walls. Good. Well, what's the trouble?'

'The Emperor Napoleon Bonaparte—'

'Ah!' Dr Bonaccord scribbled a note. 'You're really convinced of it, are you?'

Sir Lancelot screwed round his head. 'I beg your pardon?'

'Is the whole thing systematized? Do you suppose I'm Baron Larrey, who did all your amputations at Borodino? Have you been brooding much recently on Waterloo?'

'I don't think I follow?'

'Napoleon. That's who you think you are?'

'I do *not* think I am Napoleon, nor anyone else.'

The psychiatrist looked disappointed. He had suffered under Sir Lancelot as a student, and felt that had the old boy started to develop delusions of grandeur they would have to be of great magnificence to be recognized as at all abnormal.

'Cats,' said Sir Lancelot.

'Cats? By all means. Do go on.'

'The Emperor Napoleon Bonaparte suffered from a pathological terror of cats.'

'Yes, that is quite correct, according to the history books. It's not an uncommon phobia. Field-Marshal Lord Roberts in the First World War had the same trouble. He couldn't bear to be in the same room with one.'

'You may count me among that distinguished company.'

The psychiatrist's eyes glistened with interest. 'How long have you noticed this?'

'I suppose in the mildest of ways all my life. But recently it has become acute. You know my housekeeper, Miss MacNish? About four weeks ago – I remember distinctly, it was the afternoon of the students' May ball – she imported into her flat a couple of stray cats. They are a pair of highly unprepossessing animals. One is grey and thin, the other black and fat. I suspect they suffer from the mange and similar feline ailments. At first I had only a vague uneasiness in the presence of these disgusting beasts –'

Sir Lancelot paused, unable to suppress a shiver. 'The condition has steadily grown worse. Yesterday morning I suffered complete demoralization when I discovered one asleep behind the heated towel-rail as I left my bath. I can understand perfectly well how they made Napoleon feel about as imperial as a fruit jelly. They get all over my house, of course. Cats are completely impossible animals to confine. I anyway only have to *imagine* one is in the room, to suffer symptoms of the most painful anxiety. Well, Bonaccord? What's to be done about it?'

'This is of course part of the obsessional symptomatology –'

'I pray you not to beguile me with the delightfully exculpatory theories of Freud.'

'Well, how about tranquillizers?'

'For me or the cats?'

'Or wouldn't it be simpler just to change your housekeeper?'

'My dear man! Do you imagine I am going to deprive myself of the best cook in London? I am not a glutton, but a man of my age and respectability is sadly restricted in his choice of indulgences.'

'We could try some transference therapy. Excellent results have been reported recently in the journals, by bringing patients under the influence

RICHARD GORDON

of hypnosis or sodium amytal right up against the feared objects – cats, goldfish, bus-conductresses or whatever.' Sir Lancelot continued to look bleakly unenthusiastic. 'Though with a man of your well-integrated personality we could move more simply. You must simply engender feelings of tenderness towards the cats. Stroke them. Pet them. Offer them saucers of milk.'

'I could no more bring myself to touch one of those monsters than to pet a hyena with rabies.'

Dr Bonaccord looked pained again. As he had anticipated, the consultation was a trying one. 'May I finish? You can achieve this quite simply by telling yourself they are not cats at all.'

'What are they, then? Leprechauns in fur coats?'

'Babies. Human babies.'

Sir Lancelot's expression was doubtful. 'I am not particularly fond of babies.'

'Nevertheless, you'll find it works. I can absolutely guarantee it. Next time you see one of those cats, say to yourself, "What a bonnie, dear baby! I must tickle its little tum-tum." You'll be surprised how different you feel at once. We have no fear of the young of our own species.'

Sir Lancelot grunted. 'Worth a try, I suppose.'

'Most certainly. I've had very good results with people like yourself, who are stuck in the anal stage – '

'Kindly do not be disgusting.'

'I am using the term in its psychological sense,' said Dr Bonaccord quickly. 'The preoccupation with the nipple – '

He broke off, with a sharp intake of breath. Sir Lancelot looked round in concern, to see him white-faced, clutching his middle. 'I say, Bonaccord, are you all right? Or have you got this cat thing, too?'

'Just…just my heartburn. It often comes on when I'm suffering psychological strain.'

'Oh?' Sir Lancelot abruptly stood up. 'And how long have you been having that?'

'The last few weeks. It's nothing serious.'

'I wouldn't be too sure of that. Park yourself in this chair. I'll take a look at it.'

'You really needn't trouble – '

'Come along, man! You don't want to perforate a duodenal ulcer in the middle of a psychoanalysis, do you?' More reluctant patients than Dr Bonaccord had quailed under the command of Sir Lancelot's eye. He submissively lay on the chair, undoing the waistband of his trousers. Sir Lancelot deftly bared him from ribs to pubis, and laid a hand on his paunchy abdomen. 'Hurt?'

'Ooooo!'

'H'm. Could be a p.u.'

'It won't mean an operation, will it?'

'What's the odds? It'll do you a lot of good.' Sir Lancelot always made it sound like a summer holiday.

'You may think I'm terribly stupid, but…well, I have the most intense, if highly unreasonable, fear of anyone cutting me up.'

'You mean, you're stuck in the anal stage, too?'

'I know it's ridiculous. I've tried to overcome it. By transference, you understand. Like you and the cats. Telling myself surgery's some sort of clever conjuring trick, resembling sawing a lady in half.'

Sir Lancelot shot his cuffs. 'I don't think I need get my knife into you just yet. A case for medical rather than surgical treatment, I should have thought. You'd better see a physician. Why not step next door and consult the dean? He may be a miserable old sod as a neighbour, but at least he knows his way up and down the alimentary canal.'

Dr Bonaccord did up his trousers, looking relieved. 'Perhaps I'll call this evening. It may just be the matter of a suitable diet, surely? I eat rather irregularly and unwisely, being a bachelor.'

'Doesn't Mrs Tennant lend a hand?'

'My secretary keeps to her own flat,' the psychiatrist said primly.

'H'm,' said Sir Lancelot. That's not what the St Swithin's students think, he reflected. But he supposed if a medical man shared his house with an attractive young woman separated from her husband, he couldn't be blamed for putting a respectable face on it. 'Well, I'll take your tip about the cats.'

'Come back and see me tomorrow afternoon. Meanwhile, tenderness,' repeated the psychiatrist, stuffing in his shirt-tails. '*Tenderness*. You must grow to love those cats. Let them rub themselves against you. Let them walk over you. Let them sleep at the end of your bed.'

'I shall do my best,' said Sir Lancelot gamely. 'Though I should prefer the affair to remain somewhat platonic, as the pair are undoubtedly heavily infested with fleas.'

4

The dean hailed a taxi outside the main gate of St Swithin's. He would not after all be lunching in the hospital refectory that Monday. For once, he was sorry that he wouldn't be meeting Sir Lancelot. Nothing can engender such a pleasant glow in a man who for years has been dominated by another, than the secret knowledge that he has the fellow's obituary in his pocket.

The dean had intended posting it to the editor that very morning, but so many little improvements kept edging into his mind. He could for instance change the passage about Sir Lancelot's teaching methods – *undeniably effective, if reminiscent of a Victorian admiral addressing midshipmen on the quarterdeck* – to, *reminiscent of a fearless sergeant-major conducting bayonet practice.* And there was something to be squeezed in about, *he regarded life as one long after dinner, with himself the principal speaker.* He would put it in his desk drawer for a while. Time would only lighten the task, which was like trying to review some spectacular and noisy performance well before the final curtain.

'The Crécy Hotel,' he ordered the driver. His lunch with the Member of Parliament had been fixed for that very day. Frankie Humble was not one to let grass grow under anyone's feet.

The Crécy Hotel overlooking Hyde Park was one of the crop like concrete asparagus which had shot up in central London over the past five years. The dean had been there only once before, to a party of American neurophysiologists, and had thought the prices outrageous. He went through the stylish lobby to the porter's desk.

'Dr Humble?' he asked. 'I'm Sir Lionel Lychfield.'

'Dr Humble has a table in the Starlight Room, sir. The page will show you to the lift.'

When the lift doors opened on the top floor, the dean recognized his professional colleague instantly, even from the rear. No one but Frankie would lunch indoors in a three-foot cartwheel hat of pink and white tulle trimmed with yellow artificial roses.

'Lionel, my *darling*! So delighted you could make it. Was it an awful inconvenience?'

'It is never an inconvenience meeting you, Frankie.' The dean drew on forgotten stores of gallantry as he sat opposite, beside a window overlooking London.

'Sweet man. Have a vodka martini. It's all I allow myself these days. At home, I put a millilitre of vermouth in with a syringe. Weight, you know. These cruel contradictions of life! Eating and obesity, idleness and poverty, love and pregnancy. You must tell me all the latest scandal from dear St Swithin's. How's Sir Lancelot?'

'Dead,' said the dean sombrely.

'What!'

'I mean…not yet. But nearer to it, obviously. That is, nearer than yesterday. Or come to that, than the day before.'

'You *are* gloomy! You'd better get that glassful down your gullet and have a refill.'

Dr Frances Humble MP took a gulp of her third vodka, with onion, not olive. She was tall, fair and sunburnt, and in the ten years since captaining the St Swithin's tennis and golf teams had lost nothing of the look of being instantly ready to strip off and play any vigorous game that anybody cared to suggest. Like many other medical persons, she had turned to politics as a means of expressing even more fully a natural inclination to make people do what she thought good for them. The dean had admired her since her first professional job as his house-physician – she had seemed so intelligent, so definite, so clean-living and so efficient at everything she cared to indulge in. She was just like his daughter Muriel. Frankie also had small, soft blonde hairs covering her strong, brown forearms, which every time the dean had noticed them for years gave him a hot feeling in the back of the neck.

'And how's the political scene?' he asked, as the waiter brought his second drink.

'Much the same,' she told him gaily. 'Isn't it remarkable, however many elections we hold the same people seem to bounce to the top, all wearing their broad grins and holding their gin-and-tonics?'

The dean sighed. To any scientist, the ramshackle, haphazard machine of politics was incomprehensible. 'I often wish I could make some sense out of the manoeuvring of the world's rulers.'

'But so do I! Political life's so full of contradictions. We have socialist millionaires. We have God knows how many Tories living on the old age pension. The rich nations get richer and the poor ones poorer – though admittedly the lamentations about it in the better newspapers are very touching. Our economy pours out a cascade of total inessentials, and men will commit murder to acquire more of them. Quite mad. We only enjoy peace, perfect peace, because war has at last become efficient enough to have a reasonable promise of killing absolutely everybody. The quenelles of lobster here are perfectly delicious. I do hope you'll start with them?'

'Thank you. But I mustn't drink any more.'

'You're seeing patients this afternoon?'

'No, but I have a lot of important administrative work at St Swithin's.'

'I'm sure you could do that with your eyes shut. After all, you are one of the greatest deans in the history of the hospital.'

'Thank you.'

'Even when I was your houseman, I was staggered by your ruthless efficiency as an administrator.'

'Thank you.'

'Yet you manage to be such an utterly delightful person at the same time.'

'Thank you.'

'You know, Lionel, what an enormously tender spot I've always had for you?'

'Thank you. How's your husband?'

'Didn't you see in the paper? Just left on a trade mission to South America. He'll be away six weeks.'

'Ah.'

'It's awfully dreary, alone in the flat.'

'I'm sure.'

'Particularly in the evenings.'

'Quite.'

'Have another vodka.'

'Thank you. I mean, no.'

'Of course you will. Waiter!'

She was wearing a smart red sleeveless dress, and as she summoned the wine waiter the sunlight caught the little hairs on her forearms. The dean felt as though someone had applied an old-fashioned kaolin poultice just above his collar.

'Dear Lionel.' She gave the smile which had so often flashed across tennis-nets after administering someone a trouncing. 'I need your help. No, it's more than that. It is *you alone* who can save me.'

'Oh?'

'Lionel, *do* try and talk instead of emitting noises. You know how interested I have become in education?'

'An admirable preoccupation in any politician.'

'Well, it's a good line. We must all have one, of course,' she continued cheerfully. 'It's a quite heartening sight these days, seeing so many professional do-gooders on the make. Against pollution, for instance. Or for consumer protection. They're the latest-model bandwagons. But the voters will get tired of them. People have filthy habits naturally, and only worry about mucking up their environment through feelings of guilt, in this age of excruciating self-indulgence. As for consumer protection – well, selling anything from a beggar's box of matches upwards has always had a robust element of cheap-jackery in it. I think people rather enjoy being slightly diddled, if it's done with style. But education will go on forever. People will never think they can get enough of it – like leisure, the poor dear deluded fools.'

The dean was feeling confused with this brisk political analysis. 'What do you want me to do? Present the prizes at some secondary modern?'

'Lionel, you have a charmingly modest view of your talents.' The waiter set down his third drink. 'I get the barman to make those with genuine Soviet vodka, of course – so much stronger. No, Lionel. As dean of St

Swithin's you have gone far in the educational world. I want you to go further. Much further. Ah, here's the head waiter. Let's order. I'll tell you what I've in mind for you when we've finished eating. You look as though you could do with a good meal, I must say. Quite peaky, in fact. Is that wonderful Miss MacNish of yours off form?'

'She has been seduced by Sir Lancelot.'

'What a shame. And Josephine never did claim to shine in the kitchen, did she? I adore *cordon bleu* cooking, of course. Such a pity you didn't wait a few years and marry me instead.'

The warm feeling spread up to the dean's scalp and down his backbone. He suddenly felt quite frightened of himself. He was of course a devoted husband and family man…but it was not only in the kitchen that Josephine might shine less brilliantly than the lithe, blonde, tigerish lady running her eye critically down the menu.

'My God, you *do* look hungry,' she said, glancing up.

Frankie designedly kept the dean waiting until his coffee and brandy before returning to the reason for her invitation to lunch.

'Lionel, have you thought of your future?'

'I don't think I have one. I have achieved all I set myself to do.'

'Then I offer you new worlds to conquer, my dear little Alexander the Great. What would be your next step up from dean?'

'There simply isn't one.' He thought a moment. 'Except to be vice-chancellor of a university.'

'Exactly.'

The dean sat up. 'But that has been something quite beyond my wildest dreams.'

'But you'd make a splendid vice-chancellor. If you can handle the St Swithin's students, you can handle anyone. You would have to move house, of course.'

'Oh, I shouldn't mind in the least,' said the dean warmly.

'And resign from St Swithin's completely.'

'A pang, but soon assuaged.'

'And give up the practice of medicine.'

'Like yourself.'

'Might I take it, then, you'd accept an official offer?'

'You might well.'

'Good. Then a Ministerial announcement will be made, a week today, next Monday. I'm on the university senate, of course. I was given responsibility for sounding you out. We may be a comparatively new university, but that, don't you think, only widens the scope for impressing upon it your own ideas, your own methods, your own *personality*, Lionel.'

The dean was aware through the brandy fumes of some item vaguely worrying him. 'But which university does it happen to be?'

'Hampton Wick.'

The dean clutched the tablecloth.

'What's the matter, Lionel? Dyspepsia?'

'No...it's just that...you did say Hampton Wick?'

'Very convenient for central London. You won't miss your friends, the theatres, that sort of thing. Is that really the time? I must fly. I must be at a conference on mental health by two-thirty. Where's the waiter? Be a dear and pay the bill, will you? I'll send you a cheque later. The letter of appointment will be in the post tonight. Do give my love to Josephine. What a pity you lost that nice Miss MacNish. Everything will go very smoothly, and I can hardly wait for your inaugural address to the students next October. Do look after yourself. Bye.'

The dean sat gripping the tablecloth. 'Hampton Wick!' he muttered. 'My God, what have I done? What have I done?'

5

To slice away the elegant if faintly pseudo-Georgian front of Lazar Row at six-thirty that Monday, revealing the smallish rooms inside like a dolls' house, would expose to a warm, bright London evening three separate but overpowering crises in the lives of its inhabitants.

In the downstairs front sitting-room of No 1, Dr Bonaccord was stretched, groaning softly, on a large sofa with broad pink and orange stripes. His head lay on a wafer-like cushion in white silk. At his feet was another crystal vase, jammed with yellow and white carnations. On the white hessian-covered wall hung an oil painting of violently coloured spikes. In the corners stereo speakers played Mendelssohn's violin concerto, very quietly. His eyes were closed behind his glasses, his shirt was pulled out and the waist of his trousers opened, to expose his pink, plump abdomen with his secretary perched beside him gently massaging it.

'Better, Cedric?'

'Go on,' he murmured.

'That hurt?'

'Mmm...a little. Though I think I rather like it.' His mouth opened. She leant down to kiss him tenderly. He kept his eyes shut.

'Perhaps it wasn't such an ill-wind which blew in Sir Lancelot today, Gisela? I've been meaning to see somebody about this damn dyspepsia for a long time – far too long. It was really utterly and stupidly unprofessional of me to keep putting it off. But of course all doctors are hopeless patients.'

'Sir Lancelot's a funny old fogey, isn't he?'

Dr Bonaccord opened his eyes. 'My dear, he's *quite* unbalanced. Those outbursts of his are perfectly psychotic. I'd put him down as a cyclothyme with a strong tendency to hypomania and paranoid delusions. The most unreliable temperament for a surgeon – absolutely dangerous, in fact! Perhaps it was as well that he felt his age, or whatever he did feel, and carries on in semi-retirement. Incidentally, he has a perfectly insulting opinion of psychiatrists, which he hasn't even the good manners to try and hide.'

'So many people are the same, dear.'

Dr Bonaccord gave a deep sigh. 'Our unfortunate image is so terribly enduring. You know, a man with a beard and a thick mid-European accent, obviously far madder than the patient. The public think we're supernatural magicians or – more comfortingly – mere clowns. It's the same bivalent attitude towards anyone they're really scared of, I suppose.' Gisela went on stroking his stomach with her long fingers. 'Do you know, in Vienna – the very seed-bed from which phobias, obsessions, complexes and all the rest were transplanted into the heads of the world – there isn't a statue to Freud? To Mozart, Beethoven, a dozen composers, yes. Where's their sense of values?'

'How I loved it, our holiday in Vienna,' she said softly. 'That wonderful Hofburg Palace, where you imagined it alive with horses and soldiers in the heyday of Franz Josef.'

'Before Vienna was just the guillotined head of a dead empire.'

'That dreamy music. Those scrumptious chocolate cakes.'

'And yet, what a splendid thing it is to be a psychiatrist.' He made a slight, languid gesture towards the other houses. 'I know more about the busy minds of my neighbours than their owners do. I could match motives to the dean's simplest actions which would outrage and quite disgust him. Even the tatters of men's dreams, screwed up every daybreak to go bouncing back along the corridors of memory…once unravelled, they mean far more to *me* than to the dreamers. *I* know of the swirling currents under the floorboards of their consciousness, which affect them more than they could imagine possible, like the subterranean sewers the inhabitants of medieval houses. *I* have cracked the strange codes of human thought – you've stopped massaging.'

'My fingers have got cramp.'

'Yet people just don't understand the simplest psychological concepts.

Do you know, Sir Lancelot simply laughed in St Swithin's the other day when I explained the lucky horseshoe represents the female genitalia. Yet it's so obvious when you think about it. If only people could be *reasonable* and *normal*.' He gave a long, low whistling sigh. 'Like me. All *I* crave is a little simple affection and tenderness – don't I? I honestly believe I am one of the very few perfectly balanced men in the entire world, psychologically.'

She kissed him again, this time with a quick flutter of her tongue against his domed forehead.

'I think I *will* look in and see the old dean about my stomach, once he gets home. I'll hear him come in, of course. These houses are really dreadfully jerry-built. The hospital should have spent much more money on them.'

'They're delightfully cheap to rent.'

Dr Bonaccord fell silent for a moment. 'Remember that job I was offered last week, away from St Swithin's? Perhaps I turned it down rather hastily, just because it wasn't in clinical psychiatry. I think we should move from here, Gisela.'

'But why?'

'People may suspect something about us.'

She looked indignant. 'I've got my own flat, haven't I?'

'Oh, yes…but…well, remember how old Sir Lancelot looked at us under his eyebrows, when we were dancing rather indiscreetly at the students' May Ball?'

'We'd drunk too much of his champagne.'

'Or perhaps people simply expect us to get married? Divorce is so easy these days.'

'I must have explained a thousand times how my husband is abroad, and very difficult.'

'Well, maybe it's safe to stay. Tickle me. No, not with your fingers. As I like it.'

She slipped off her shoes, climbed on to the sofa, balanced herself astride him, hitched her skirt above her hips and tickled his right ear with her nylon-sheathed big toe, 'Nice?'

'Lovely.' There was a crash from next door. 'That's the dean coming home. He had lunch with Frances Humble today.'

'How do you know?'

'I met her at this afternoon's session of the seminar on student mental health.'

There were more noises from next door. The dean seemed to be rampaging through the house shouting his head off. Dr Bonaccord took Gisela's foot, and putting her big toe in his mouth sucked it for some moments contemplatively. Then she resumed gently tickling his ear with it. He always thought it felt nicer when it was moist.

6

'Josephine!' The dean flung open his bedroom door. 'Josephine!' He went
back to the landing and shouted down the staircase. 'Josephine! Where are
you?'

There was no reply. 'Damn,' muttered the dean. He had a bad
headache and a taste as though his mouth was filled with iron filings.
'Where is the bloody woman?'

He heard the front door shut again. 'There you are, Josephine. Where
the devil had you got to?'

She looked alarmed as he hurried downstairs into the narrow hall. 'I
was only posting a letter. I wanted to catch the late collection from the box
outside St Swithin's.'

'How did I manage to miss you? I've just come from the hospital.' The
dean led her into the front room on the ground floor. The walls of their
sitting-room were half-covered with bookcases, there was a painting of St
Swithin's in the eighteenth century on one wall and an etching of the
dean's Cambridge college on the other, at the far end a glass case with the
silver cups he had won for running as a student. He threw himself on to a
comfortable shabby sofa of flowered chintz, head on a green satin cushion
extruding its feathers, feet stretched towards an occasional table with a
pink cyclamen. 'Something terrible has happened.'

'It's the students – they've put the matron's car on the roof again?'

'No, no...though I'll never object in future to a little bit of harmless,
innocent clean fun like that. Do sit down, Josephine. You're irritating me,
striding about.'

She sat in a velvet-covered armchair and folded her hands expectantly.

39

'I met Frankie Humble for lunch.'

'Was she as pressingly charming as ever?'

'She offered me a job. Vice-chancellor of a new university.'

Josephine jumped up. 'But how absolutely thrilling!'

'Of Hampton Wick University.'

'Oh!' She sat down again.

'It's been founded…how long? Barely five years. And it's got through ten vice-chancellors.' He gave a hollow laugh. 'Each of them appointed for life.'

'Poor Bill Smeed was always in delicate health, remember.'

'Oh, yes. But not so delicate that he had to go on a world cruise to recover after only three months, I suppose they should never have exposed a meek little civil servant to those terrible students. He was followed by the clerical fellow, Canon Grimes. As far as I know, he's still in that mental home. The next was the Australian, who simply packed his bags after a couple of nights and went back to Melbourne. Wise fellow. Then Professor Dancer – '

'Dear man! I grew quite fond of him, visiting him in the wards at St Swithin's before he died.'

'And the final outrage on the economist fellow, Dumble – '

'Perhaps the newspapers played it up, dear. They always do.'

The dean snorted. 'At Hampton Wick, they don't need to exaggerate. I suppose it's fair game for the students, occupying the vice-chancellor's private house for six weeks, But making him wait on them hand and foot, cleaning out the lavatories – '

'Better than being tarred and feathered four Saturdays running, like the Canon.'

'They don't need a vice-chancellor. They need a particularly conscientious commandant from a Siberian salt mine.'

'But the students there might like you, dear.'

'How? Fried, I suppose. That almost happened to Bill Smeed. They set the place on fire, then chopped the firemen's hoses with axes and drove the engines to London for an evening out.'

'I admit, Lionel, the undergraduates sound something of a problem.'

'They're the most undisciplined bunch of roughnecks in the country –

in the entire world, I should imagine. Academic Mafia. They actually *revel* in their awful reputation. All those well-meaning people who have accepted invitations to speak at Hampton Wick...' The dean shuddered. 'The Thames must be silted up with their motorcars by now.'

Josephine persisted grimly in seeing the bright side. 'But just think, the university's all beautifully modern, and we'll have a delightful free house – if they can ever evict the sitting-in students, of course.'

'I won't do it. I refuse to preside over a non-stop carnival of promiscuity, psychopathy, pregnancy, and pot.'

'So you didn't accept?'

The dean hesitated. 'I did.'

'Lionel! How could you, when you hated the very idea?'

'Well...you know how Frankie is when she wants her own way.'

'You're an absolute fool. You always behave towards Frankie like a first-year student to the first junior nurse who bothers to smile at him.'

The dean looked offended. 'On the contrary. I admire Frankie only for her intellect.'

'Nonsense. It's all sex.'

The dean fell silent, scowling at the cyclamen. 'Anyway, what the devil am I going to do?'

'Tell her you've changed your mind.'

'Tell Frankie? She'd soon change it back again.'

'Suggest someone else for the post.'

'My dear Josephine, nobody in the entire academic world would touch that job with a well-sterilized barge-pole. I suppose that's the only reason she asked me,' he added ruefully.

'Surely you can think of someone? Another doctor, perhaps? One older than you, who's retiring anyway, who wouldn't worry overmuch if he only lasted a few months? There must be *someone* with the knack of enjoying popularity among the students – even if it's a cheap popularity.'

'I can't think of a soul. I certainly wouldn't recommend Hampton Wick to one of my friends. I don't think I'd care to offer it even to my worst enemy...'

There was a violent thumping noise from the wall on the dean's left. 'Really! These houses are ridiculous. It's bad enough hearing that peculiar fellow Bonaccord playing records or scraping away on the violin till all hours, but living next door to Sir Lancelot is like being on top of an Army assault course—'

The dean paused. He slowly scratched his chin. For the first time a faintly cheerful expression came to his face. 'I wonder... I wonder...' he muttered to himself. 'Well, it would certainly make an awfully good end to his obituary.

7

The thump which had disturbed the dean was Sir Lancelot hurling a copy of *Progress in Clinical Surgery* at the crimson velvet curtain which hung from a brass rail to cover his sitting-room door. He stood on the Indian rug in the middle of the polished floor, breathing heavily. He shuddered, producing again the red-and-white spotted handkerchief to mop his face. But nothing emerged from behind the door curtain. There was no movement. No mewing. 'Imagination,' muttered Sir Lancelot. 'I mustn't let it get me down. I can conquer this thing. Just as I've conquered a lot of other unfortunate little traits in my life, like going into an abdomen too late and striking at a trout too early.'

He sat again in the deep leather armchair. His sitting-room resembled the corner of a comfortable club, with plain walls of battleship grey, some early nineteenth-century prints of angling scenes and two enormous brown trout in glass cases, glassy-eyed and lacquered, to Sir Lancelot as emotive a reminder of past glories as the equally carefully preserved contents of the Kremlin mausoleum to the population of Moscow. At his left elbow was an angled reading-lamp, at his right a small table with the folded *Times* and *Lancet*, and a half-finished large whisky and soda with decanter and syphon, on a silver tray laid out by Miss MacNish. On his knee was a blotter, with the foolscap pages of the dean's obituary.

Sir Lancelot was in a mellow, indulgent frame of mind as the whisky gently ironed the wrinkles out of his soul. The consultation with the nut-wallah Bonaccord had not proved too painful – possibly his advice might even be worth taking. Neither cat had appeared all day, and he was even entertaining the cheerful notion that they had both been squashed somewhere by a bus. And there was tripe and onions for dinner – though inclined to produce wind in the bowel, certainly a dish to savour in anticipation. Sir Lancelot twitched his nostrils as the delicate, delicious scent pierced the door-curtain. His eye ran along the handwritten lines on his knee. The dean wasn't really such a bad sort at heart, he decided. He took out his fountain-pen and changed, *Lychfield's natural abstemiousness was unfortunately interpreted by his friends as a certain meanness in sociability* to *His aesthetic streak happily did not prevent him from accepting with cheerfulness the hospitality of others.*

Sir Lancelot suddenly looked up. For almost a minute he sat stock-still, staring across the room over his half-moon glasses. Then with a deliberate movement he set pen and obituary on the side-table. He stood up. 'I shall overcome,' he murmured. 'I shall definitely overcome,'

He stared round keenly. This time it wasn't his fancy. There was one about somewhere.

'Am I a man?' he asked himself sombrely. 'Or indeed a mouse?'

He stood stroking his beard, shuddering slightly. Perhaps it would have been easier, he thought, had he succumbed to the temptation of slipping poison into the tins of well-advertised cat food which Miss MacNish put out with the same attention as she laid his dinner. Something rather painful, like strychnine. But that would have been unsporting. It was more humane to try the psychological cure, if less likely to be immediately effective.

'Puss,' Sir Lancelot said bravely. 'Pretty puss.'

Something moved. It was in the nook between a small bookcase and the corner. Sir Lancelot felt his hands tremble. Then like some old soldier, battleweary but screwing up his courage, he pursed his lips and uttered a moist squeaking noise. The cat appeared with callous insouciance round the bookcase, tail high. At least it was Chelsea the black one, not Kensington the grey one, which Sir Lancelot liked even less.

'Pussy-wussy,' said Sir Lancelot.

It sat, staring at him with yellow eyes.

'Tenderness,' said Sir Lancelot. '*Tenderness.*'

He advanced gingerly across the rug. The cat started washing itself. The long pink tongue made Sir Lancelot remember saucers of milk, and he wondered distractedly if whisky and soda would do instead. 'Think of it as a baby,' he told himself. He bravely extended a hand. 'Nice little baby. Tickleum tum-tums.'

The cat abandoned its toilet and gave a haughty glare. Sir Lancelot crouched down and touched it. The cat arched its back, stuck out its tail, and made a noise like the final squirt from a soda-syphon.

'Ahhhhhh!' cried Sir Lancelot.

He leapt back, knocking over the table and smashing the decanter. To keep his balance he grabbed the reading lamp, tripped over the flex, and plunged beside the armchair. 'Bloody animal!' he shouted. 'Pestiferous beast!'

The cat resumed licking itself. The door flew open and Miss MacNish appeared.

'Sir Lancelot! Are you all right?'

'Of course I am *not* all right. Do you imagine I have been entertaining a poltergeist, or something?'

She hastened to help him up. 'But what was the matter?'

Sir Lancelot jabbed a forefinger. '*That* was the matter. That articulated flue-brush.'

A chilly look frosted the warm solicitude of her expression. 'Do I take it that you don't care for my cat?'

'I have no feelings one way or another about the animal. I only ask you to keep it permanently out of my sight, that's all.'

Miss MacNish knelt to pick up the broken decanter. 'You can't expect cats to stay imprisoned all day in my little flat,'

'Why not? I'll buy a couple of birdcages for them if you like.'

'I was always brought up to believe one should be kind to dumb animals.'

'But those cats aren't dumb.' Chelsea had hollowed its back and was sharpening its claws on the door-curtain. 'They may not actually *say* anything, but they radiate malevolence like an atomic pile.'

Her lips were tight. 'I simply don't understand you, Sir Lancelot. I really don't.'

'Get it out of here, before it has the door-curtain in ribbons.'

Miss MacNish stood up. 'You're *always* being nasty to my cats,' she burst out.

'On the contrary, they're always being extremely unpleasant to me.'

45

'Yes, you are. Ever since I gave the poor wee things a home. You think you haven't noticed, don't you? But I have. Yes indeed, I have. I saw you tread on poor Kensington. *Tread on her*, with your great big feet. And just now, I heard you throw something at Chelsea. If I so much as told the RSPCA, there'd be a fine old scandal in the Sunday papers.'

'My dear Miss MacNish! I assure you I enjoy humane feelings towards mankind and all warm-blooded creatures—'

'Oh, I know you medical people. You'll take my cats over to the hospital and do unspeakable things if you have half the chance. I've read all about vivisection, you know.' She gathered the fragile bones of contention and pressed them to her bosom. 'There, there! Poor little harmless beastie. Was the man nasty to you, then? Dinner is served,' she added briskly, disappearing.

Sir Lancelot snorted. He felt the only dish for which he now had appetite was a brace of roast cat. He glanced sadly at the whisky-stain on the rug, then went through another door to the small dining-room, containing a couple more stuffed fish. Miss MacNish came in with a large steaming, china tureen, a silver spoon protruding through its lid.

'Miss MacNish, I think I owe you an explanation. I am, in fact, delighted you have those two animals as your companions – you must become somewhat bored up there, with nothing but the television. And doubtless they are admirable examples of their species. My behaviour can be explained perfectly simply, in that I suffer a sort of psychological allergy to cats. I cannot bear to be within yards of one. It's like being with...well, something entirely disgusting and menacing. Something like a venomous snake. Many distinguished men have felt exactly the same,' he added quickly. 'It was possibly a cat straying into Napoleon's tent at Waterloo which changed the course of European history.'

Miss MacNish plonked the tripe in the middle of the table. 'Disgusting and menacing are they?'

'I only meant they affect *me* that way,' he said patiently.

'I'm glad that at least you admit I might get bored in the evenings.' He noticed two bright red patches on her freckled cheeks. 'But a lot you care about that, don't you. When have you asked me down for a chat? Or a glass of whisky? When? Even on Christmas Day you didn't.'

'My dear Miss MacNish, you must surely see that sort of thing would be most improper for a man on his own.'

'Oh? A scarlet woman, am I? Going to seduce you on your own hearthrug in ten minutes before I cook your dinner? Thank you. Now I know exactly where I stand in your estimation.'

'Damnation, woman! I did not mean that in the slightest –'

'Please do not become uncivil.'

'Can't you understand? I greatly appreciate your services –'

'You don't. Not like the dean did. Never a kind word comes out of you from one year's end to another. I want to cook lovely things for you, and what do you ask for? Tripe!'

'But what in the name of God has all this to do with the cats? Miss MacNish – Fiona. Don't you remember those days when you were a young girl just down from Aberdeen? When I gave you a job as my Harley Street receptionist?'

'And worked the hide off my back for a pittance. You took advantage of my innocence to exploit me. Still, if you imagined I'd the outlook of some girl in the white slave trade –'

'You're bloody impossible –'

'Besides, you have a large number of very unpleasant habits. You leave your trousers crumpled on the floor, and the curly hairs at the bottom of the bath –'

'I am going to eat my dinner.'

Sir Lancelot sat down. There was a loud squawk. Kensington, the grey one, flew from underneath him. Sir Lancelot jumped up. He swung his toe and caught it hard in the soft fur of the abdomen,

'You vile beast!'

Miss MacNish picked up the casserole. Sir Lancelot ducked as she threw it, but it shattered on the wall behind, spattering hot white liquid everywhere. Then she burst into tears, left the room, and stumped furiously upstairs.

8

The dean looked up as he heard the crash against the wall.

'Ah, tut!' He wrinkled his nose. The noise was bad enough, but it was more unpleasant always to be smelling Sir Lancelot's meals, which seemed to consist entirely of onions. He turned back to the foolscap on his knee as a door slammed violently in the next house. 'Dear me, dear me,' muttered the dean. 'Altogether, it's like living in the back streets of Naples.' It would be so much more agreeable if Sir Lancelot could be persuaded to leave, he thought. Indeed, it seemed to be becoming essential.

He clicked down his ballpoint. Scoring through a line, he substituted, *Sir Lancelot's usual inflexibility was, however, broken by the adroit persuasion of close colleagues, and he was fortunate in spending his final years in academic serenity as vice-chancellor of the University of Hampton Wick.*

Another door slammed beyond the wall, rattling the collection of silver running cups. The dean began to think urgently how best to persuade Sir Lancelot to accept the academic hot potato. Any offer originating from himself would at once arouse suspicion, hostility and even derision. He supposed he could play on Sir Lancelot's popularity with the St Swithin's students – though he felt the rugby club kept the surgeon as their president only to trundle him out at inter-hospital matches with their other mascot, a stuffed gorilla. The invitation would best come in a roundabout way, from some third party. The dean tapped the ballpoint against his front teeth. Why not Frankie herself? She would certainly agree to the change of candidate, if she thought there was a sound chance of hooking him. He knew she was fond of Sir Lancelot, for whom she had once worked as house-surgeon after leaving his own medical unit. Though not so fond as of myself, thought the dean with a smile. His mind went back to another students' May ball, the year Frankie had been president of the union. Little did Sir Lancelot – or anyone else – know exactly what had happened in the dark behind the bandstand. If word of such behaviour had leaked out –

The sitting-room door was flung open. His daughter Muriel strode across the threshold.

'Yes? What is it?' He was irritated at losing such an agreeable train of thought. 'I'm busy for the moment on Sir Lancelot's ob–' The dean hastily checked himself. 'Obturator foramen. I'm doing an anatomical sketch for him.'

'Where's Mother?'

'In the kitchen getting dinner, of course.' Muriel remained standing, one hand on the door-handle. 'Do come in, my dear, or go out. It's extremely draughty.'

'Can I have a word with you, Father? Alone?'

'Yes, of course. But do make it sharpish. As I said, I'm very busy on Sir Lancelot's obit – *obiter dicta*. I'm making a collection of them.'

Muriel shut the door. She stood rigidly against it, hand still grasping the knob.

'I say, are you all right?' asked the dean. 'You look rather pale.'

'Yes, I'm perfectly all right. Or rather, I'm not. I mean, I'm not ill. Everything's perfectly physiological.'

'Then I'm relieved to hear it.'

'Father... I've someone outside in the hall who wants to speak to you.'

'Well, bring her in, for God's sake. Why on earth all this fuss? It's your own home.'

'It isn't a she. It's a he. One of the students.'

'As dean of the hospital, I hardly need to be introduced to my own students.'

'No. No, of course not.'

'Which one is it?'

Muriel swallowed. 'Edgar Sharpewhistle.'

The dean looked relieved. 'I thought it was some scallawag who'd got himself into trouble, or got you into trouble, or something. You can easily get led astray by these young men, you know. You can find yourself driving without proper insurance, parking on double yellow lines, that sort of thing.'

'You're sure you feel strong enough, Father?'

'I'm always delighted to talk to such an intelligent, industrious and generally admirable student as Sharpewhistle. You know I regard him as something of a decoration to the medical school.'

She suddenly looked doubtful. 'He can come back another day, if you like.'

'Do stop havering. Bring the poor fellow in.' Muriel opened the door. Edgar Sharpewhistle came in silently and stood beside her. He looked shamefaced and pinker than ever. Both stared at the dean without speaking. 'Well,' exclaimed the dean cheerfully. 'What's the reason for this pregnant silence?'

'Errk,' said Muriel.

'What's that, my dear.'

'Nothing. Nothing, Father,'

'Well, what *is* it, Sharpewhistle?' The dean began to sound impatient. 'You've come about your cases up in the ward, I suppose? That cysticercosis in bed number six – '

'No. It isn't about that, sir.' The student seemed to be speaking with a mouth full of sawdust.

'Then it must be the dermatomyositis in bed number ten. Very interesting urinary creatinine levels. I hope you've studied the electromyograph? They're not entirely typical patterns, but perfectly clear to the astute diagnostician – as of course you are. I expect further investigation in the shape of a muscle biopsy – '

'I didn't come about the dermatomyositis, sir. I want to marry your daughter.'

The dean jumped up, open-mouthed. 'But how extraordinary.'

'What should be extraordinary about it in the slightest?' demanded Muriel.

He looked his daughter up and down, with the expression of being introduced to her for the first time in his life. He had never thought her to have the slightest interest in men. Not Sharpewhistle, nor in any man at all. He had felt this an admirable deficiency in a young woman, allowing her to concentrate on her work, to take a balanced view of life, and to practise a welcome economy in clothes and entertainments. 'I mean, isn't it extraordinarily sudden?'

'We met when we started at St Swithin's five years ago, Father. We have been in each other's company for a good part of every day since.'

'It's simply that I imagined two students of your remarkable calibre would have been concentrating on your work,' said the dean uncomfortably. 'That you'd be far too busy for any...er, hanky-panky, as we used to call sex and so on in my day.'

Sharpewhistle gave a slow smile. 'Love will always find a way, sir.'

'Even in hospital, I suppose? The ward sluice-rooms must be absolutely pregnant with possibilities.'

'Errk,' said Muriel again.

The dean rubbed his hands in a businesslike way. Though it was not a situation he had anticipated, vague ideas from his youth flickered in his mind. One asked about parentage and prospects, in that order.

'What's your father?' he asked the suitor.

'He's an actuary in Pontefract, sir.'

'Well, I'm sure that's very fascinating work. And Pontefract is probably a delightful place. They have a castle there, and cakes, don't they? What's your future like?'

'I hope to win the St Swithin's gold medal, sir.' He turned to smile at Muriel. 'Unless my fiancée does?'

'Your fiancée? Who's she? Oh, I see. Yes. Well.' The dean stopped. 'You're not going to get any financial support from me, you know. Put that out of your head for a start. I'm taxed to the bone. To the very marrow. Nor will you live with us, either. We need every inch.'

'I hope my winnings from *IQ Quiz* will pay the deposit on a small house, sir.'

The dean nodded. He did not approve of *IQ Quiz*, nor anything else on television. But it *would* be convenient to have Muriel's top-floor flat free, as a spacious study and library for himself. Apart from anything else, it would move him further from the smell of Sir Lancelot's onions. He took a closer look at his future son-in-law. The fellow was admittedly no

Adonis. Indeed, the dean wondered if he might be somewhat abnormal, an overweight achondroplastic dwarf. 'You should have extremely intellectual children,' he said in a consoling voice. 'Muriel! You're trembling.'

'Emotion, Father.'

'Do I take it you approve, then?' asked Sharpewhistle.

'Yes, I er, think, er. Yes.'

Muriel pursed her lips irritably. 'Don't you suppose Mother should be consulted as well?'

The dean started. He had quite forgotten that Josephine might have some interest in the matter. A pleasant thought brightened his face. 'I'll fetch her from the kitchen. And I believe the moment calls for champagne, doesn't it? I remember now, I put a bottle in the refrigerator last Christmas, but never seemed to get round to opening it. Or perhaps it was the Christmas before. Well, behave yourselves.'

With the coy grin to which all newly-engaged couples are subjected, suggesting they are avid to perform a variety of intimacies the instant they are left alone, the dean bounced from the sitting-room.

Sharpewhistle blew out his cheeks. 'Well, that's that, then.'

'I told you it would go all right. My father's a perfect lamb, really, when you get the hang of handling him. I can't understand why you were making so much fuss.'

'You didn't leave me much time to make up my mind, did you? It's hardly an hour since you heard your test was positive.'

'Why did you want time? I should have thought that positive result would have made up your mind for you.'

'Well, yes.' He stuck his small fat hands into his trouser pockets. 'Muriel, you're *sure* you're...you're sure you're sure about all this?' She glared at him. 'I mean, well, there are easier ways out.'

'There aren't. Or do you regard marrying me as the most excruciating of penances?'

'No, no, not that...but these days... Of course, some people do have objections to termination on religious or moral grounds. I'd be the first to respect them. But like most medical people, I don't think you or I would suffer qualms of conscience, even if perhaps we ought to.'

52

'I am not going to seek a termination. It is simply that I think it is wrong. A coward's way out. I never like starting anything that I don't intend to go through with to the end.'

'I suppose you know your own mind best,' he said uncomfortably.

'You're quite right, Edgar. I do. And when I am determined to do something, nothing in this world can divert me. You have put me in this condition, and you must marry me.'

'That's fair enough, I suppose…'

'After all, it is unlikely that any other people would ever want to marry either of us.'

'True, true…'

'While you and I are completely matched in tastes, outlook and intelligence.'

'Quite, indeed…'

'So what are you worrying about?'

'I'm not, not really.'

'Then look a bit more cheerful before Father comes back. Anyone would think you were booked to go into hospital instead of on honeymoon. We're going to be very happy.'

'Oh, I'm sure we are. Very happy indeed.'

9

'My darlings!' Josephine appeared, behind her the dean, both smiling broadly.

'This must be the coldest bottle of champagne in London.' The dean set it on the table beside Sir Lancelot's obituary, while his wife kissed the newly-betrothed pair with maternal murmurings of delight. He produced four smallish glasses from the triangular cupboard in the corner where he kept his decanter of sherry. 'I am quite delighted, Muriel my dear. And of course for you…er, what *is* your name? I can't keep calling you Sharpewhistle.'

'Edgar, sir.'

'Charming name,' said Josephine.

'Your news was something of a surprise. It was my second one today. At lunch I was handed, out of the blue, a vice-chancellorship. Of Hampton Wick University.' The dean chuckled. 'Were I superstitious, I'd be on my guard for a third shock before nightfall.' He started fiddling with the foil of the champagne cork. 'Strange, how I think of you both as very young for this momentous and very serious – indeed quite solemn – step of matrimony. I remember, I was thought no end of a dog, because your mother was a young bride. Yet of course, you're really most mature by today's standards for the process. Mind you, it's not that I approve particularly of today's standards towards marriage nor towards a great deal of other things. But I suppose it is not the doctor's job to moralize. Only to diagnose, which requires considerably more intelligence. They say young people now become sexually active earlier because they are better fed in childhood. Well, perhaps so –'

'Lionel, I'm sure they're not interested –'

'The Victorian skivvy seduced by the rascally squire was probably quite infertile, after a vitamin-deficient diet of bread and potatoes, thus saving a good deal of trouble to everybody. But today's plump, healthy girls…pop goes the weasel, as one might say, before they've mastered the three Rs. They start multiplying even before they learn their tables, eh?' He gave a laugh. 'What's that, Muriel?'

'I just coughed, Father.'

The dean went on fiddling with the champagne cork. 'Though I fancy young folk marry not because they are seized with overwhelming passion, nor inflamed by the widespread titillation of the age. It's simply that today they earn more money. They see those advertisements in the Sunday coloured supplements – all those smartly-clad people in their sleek open cars, all of them experts in food, drink and internal décor, all wife-loving, home-loving, and of course completely odourless.' He wrinkled his nose. Yes, Sharpewhistle did pong a bit. 'And what happens? Young people want these consumer durables for themselves. Nice houses, nice cars, nice wives, nice babies. Did you know that the number of women marrying under twenty-one was under sixty thousand a year before the war? While in the latest Registrar-General's returns it was no less than *one hundred and sixty-one thousand*, the largest group by ten per cent –'

'I do wish you would stop giving us a lecture, Lionel,' said his wife shortly. 'Just open that bottle of champagne. When are you thinking of the wedding, dear? After you both qualify at Christmas, I suppose.'

'No, next Monday,' said Muriel.

Josephine started. 'You seem a little eager, dear.'

'Monday?' The dean looked irritable. 'That's quite impossible. I've got a meeting.'

'It will be Monday,' Muriel repeated.

'But Muriel!' objected her mother. 'How on earth will you expect to have a wedding-dress by then? Or even a wedding-cake? And we can hardly expect our friends to come to the reception at such short notice. We couldn't even have the invitations printed. We'd have to telephone everybody, which would take absolutely days –'

'Monday.'

'Surely you *want* a white wedding, dear? Not one of these hole-and-corner businesses in a registry office?'

Muriel swallowed. 'I think a registry office would be best.'

The dean put the bottle down. 'There's no need to be secretive about it, you know. After all, a man in my position, dean of St Swithin's, Fellow of the Royal College and all that, is rather expected to put on something of a show. Half medical London will be delighted to come and drink my champagne. The expense will to some extent be justified by helping my private practice – '

'I think it would be better to have a quiet ceremony, Father. Then people won't find it so easy to remember the date.'

Josephine clasped her hands. 'But surely, your wedding day is a date to remember – '

'I am having a baby.'

'What!' The dean dropped the champagne bottle. 'You mean you're…you're… Good God!'

'How nice,' said Josephine.

'Nice?' The dean glared. 'It isn't nice at all. Not one bit.'

'Don't be stupid, Lionel. Most couples these days prefer to keep their independence by staying unmarried until the girl's in the family way.'

'It's immoral. Completely immoral.'

'Of course it isn't a matter of morals, Lionel. Only of fashion. For centuries, hard-working country girls would never have dreamed of getting married until they'd clicked.'

'Our daughter is not a bloody milkmaid.'

'I suppose we could say it was a premature baby?' suggested Muriel helpfully.

'Do you imagine anyone believes that chestnut any more?' demanded the dean angrily. 'Look at them in the Sunday papers, actresses holding premature babies the size of primary schoolchildren.' He jabbed his finger in the direction of Sharpewhistle. The young man had turned scarlet, and was pushing his back against the sitting-room wall as though anxious to break through the brickwork. 'And it's all your bloody fault.'

'At least I want to marry her, sir.'

'Marry her? You? By God, that's out of the question.'

'Lionel! Have you gone mad – '

'Absolutely out of the question.' The dean was a small man, but he could tower over Sharpewhistle. He jabbed him with his forefinger, hard on the sternum. 'How *dare* you ask to marry my daughter. You, you bounder. You cad, who goes round putting innocent girls in the family way.'

'But, sir – '

'Shut up. Get out of my house at once. I'm not at all certain I shan't want you at my office tomorrow morning, to answer for a blatant piece of student indiscipline. Thank God I didn't open the champagne!'

'Father, please be reasonable – '

'You're not much better, my girl. It takes two to make a quarrel or a baby. When did all this happen, anyway? Not under my roof, I hope.'

'It was the night of the May ball.'

'Oh? In your friend Tulip's flat? I'll have *her* in my office in the morning for sure.'

'It was in Edgar's digs. I didn't go to her flat.'

'Ah! You deceived me?'

'Well, I… I suppose I'd drunk too much champagne.'

'So you were fuddled? Half-senseless? Your inhibitions gone. A sitting target for ugly little pocket-sized predators like Sharpewhistle here. And who poured this champagne into you? I don't have to ask.' He gave a bitter laugh. 'I noticed it. Don't think I didn't. Sir Lancelot, absolutely plying you.'

'Father, why must you blame everyone in sight? Sir Lancelot was being very kind. He said a shy girl like me needed a skinful before she got in the mood.'

'Mood? What mood?'

'Sir Lancelot said that premarital relations were far less likely to kill you than smoking cigarettes, more enjoyable and much cheaper. That it was the only pleasure the Government hadn't yet got round to putting a tax on.'

'But what extraordinary advice for Sir Lancelot to volunteer to a young woman! To the daughter of his oldest and dearest friend and neighbour, into the bargain.'

'That's not fair. If you must know, I asked Sir Lancelot's advice outright, during the party. That's what he gave me.'

A door slammed. The dean spun round, staring through the window. Sir Lancelot was leaving his house, in ginger tweed knickerbockers and deerstalker, in one hand a pair of fishing-rods in cloth covers, on his back creel and net, in his other hand an overnight bag. The dean threw the window open.

'Lancelot – !'

The surgeon glared. 'Been making a lot of noise in there, haven't you? Sounds like the last act at Covent Garden.'

'I wish to speak to you.'

'Sorry, cock. I've suddenly decided to go fishing.'

'Good evening, dean. I've been ringing your bell for some time, but nobody seemed to hear it.'

The dean turned his head, to see Dr Bonaccord on his doorstep. 'What the devil do you want?'

'It was about my dyspepsia – '

'What the hell do you mean, Bonaccord, coming along at this moment of supreme crisis in my life, and talking about your horrible dyspepsia? Though as a matter of fact,' he added, 'it might not be a bad idea if you came in and took a look at my daughter. Lancelot! Don't you dare creep off like that. I demand an explanation.'

'For God's sake, dean. What's the trouble? My plumbing rumbling again, I suppose? I assure you that I have problems enough of my own.'

'Your behaviour is utterly disgraceful. I withdraw my offer of that delightful academic job.'

Sir Lancelot frowned.

'What job? In my entire life you've never offered me so much as a drink.' He started to move away.

'Stop! I want to talk about Muriel.'

'That is not a subject I choose to delay my going fishing, however delightful.'

'You have ruined her.'

'I beg your pardon?'

'That is not putting it too strongly. You are responsible for fathering my grandchild.'

Sir Lancelot stared at the psychiatrist. 'I say, Bonaccord. Be a good chap, will you? Get on to the relevant authorities and have an order made for the poor fellow to be put inside. Though if I were you, I wouldn't venture inside his house without the strongarm squad. Absolutely raving, obviously. Sorry I can't stay to help – with a bit of luck I'll be tranquillizing myself on the banks of the Kennet before it gets dark. Perhaps you'd care for a nice brace of trout?'

10

'Ah!' cried the dean. 'Not another! For God's sake, not another.'

'Lionel,' said his wife.

'That's two entire teams, a referee, and a pair of linesmen.'

'Lionel!'

The dean raised his head from the pillow. 'Dear me. I must have been having another of my dreams.'

'You were counting out loud.'

'Yes, I remember now. I was in St Swithin's and was suddenly called into the maternity department to perform a delivery. I was in a panic, as I'd absolutely forgotten all my midwifery – it was one of those awful dreams, you know, like when you're on the stage in front of a huge audience and you've no idea of your lines and stark naked into the bargain –'

'Perhaps, Lionel, you'd better go and see Dr Bonaccord after all?'

'There was the mother, groaning away and bearing down. I remember distinctly, I sat down between her legs in the lithotomy position, and the babies came popping out like rabbits from a warren –'

'To quote from my favourite book, *The Diary of a Nobody*, nothing is so completely uninteresting as other people's dreams.'

'The funny thing was their all being in football togs. There were twenty-five babies altogether. I remember distinctly thinking they were Chelsea *v* Arsenal. Strange. Must be through looking at the television on Saturdays. I can't think of any other reason for having such a strange – Oh God!'

His wife got out of bed. 'It's almost eight o'clock.'

'Josephine, I've just remembered. That ghastly business about Muriel. I suppose I didn't dream that too?' he added hopefully.

'Muriel's already left the house.'

Supported on an elbow, the dean picked irritably at the turned-down sheet. 'I wish she hadn't rushed off like that. I wanted to speak to her. I hardly had a chance last night, with her going upstairs and slamming the door.'

'Can you blame her, after you made such an exhibition of yourself?'

'She mustn't let this get round St Swithin's. It would undermine my authority with the students completely. That's difficult enough to maintain as it is.'

'I do hope she got herself some breakfast.'

'Why are you so obviously taking her side?'

'She needs all the support she can get, poor dear.' Josephine went through the door into their bathroom. The dean grunted, and lay glaring across the bedroom. He reached for his large glasses and the four sheets of paper he had been reading the night before. Taking his ballpoint, he scratched out some lines on the last page. He wrote instead. *His final years were made painful for his friends by a depravity which made him actively corrupt young persons of the other sex, instead of guiding them away from the shaming temptations of the age.* The dean got out of bed, in his blue-and-white spotted pyjamas.

'She won't have an abortion, I suppose?' the dean asked gloomily, as his wife turned off the bath-taps. 'I could easily fix it with the hospital. One needs a green form, I believe. It's the only one the gynae people say to arrive by first-class mail.'

'No, she won't.' Josephine lay splashing her good-looking legs in the water.

'I can't understand Muriel, when half the young women of Europe are flocking here for that specific purpose.' He leant against the bathroom door-post. 'Or she could have the child adopted. But no, I don't think so. I do not at all like the idea of a face which might be similar to my own amid a family of persons I do not know, nor perhaps would even care to.'

'All this scratching about is quite unnecessary, Lionel. She's going to marry Edgar.'

'She's not.'

'You're quite impossible.' Josephine soaped herself with a large yellow sponge. 'You don't like him, do you?'

'Quite frankly, I think he's a little pustule. He does all the things I find particularly distasteful in the hospital.' The dean mounted his clinical-looking bathroom scales. 'He pushes himself to the front of all my classes. He asks intelligent questions to which he already knows the answers. And he corrects my own diagnoses. That he is sometimes right and I am wrong has nothing to do with it. The students are all far too uppish these days. They're completely lacking in the basic Hippocratic art of concealing the fact they consider their teachers to be a doddering bunch of old fools.' He started fiddling with weights on the balance-arm. 'Furthermore, Sharpewhistle has an enormously inflated opinion of himself over this television quiz rubbish. He has no conversation. He is overweight. And he smells like an attendant in a sauna bath. But there's another reason Muriel isn't going to marry him. *She* doesn't like him, either.'

Josephine lay in the scented warm water in silence.

The dean inspected the balance. 'It can't be over ten stone, surely?' he murmured. 'You must agree, Josephine? If only from seeing them together last night? A girl announcing her engagement is supposed to look radiant, even in these unromantically lecherous days. Muriel only looked as she did when her wisdom teeth were giving trouble.'

'I'm afraid I *do* agree,' his wife said quietly. 'However hard I've been trying to convince myself otherwise. But…well, he is the father of her child, as they used to put it at Drury Lane.'

'She must have been out of her head to let an unprepossessing, odoriferous creature like him… Though of course, she had no control of herself at the time,' he added warmly. 'She was full of Lancelot's champagne.'

'She wasn't the only one that night, dear.'

The dean shrugged. He tapped the balance vigorously with his finger. 'It *must* be under ten stone, on my careful diet. Well, if I was a bit tiddly myself, it was only because one doesn't often get a free drink out of Lancelot, and it seemed worth making the most of it.'

Josephine pulled the bath-plug out with her toe. She gave a sudden giggle. 'When I was Muriel's age, you were always dragging me into bed, weren't you dear? Ah, well. Times have changed.'

'In those days I didn't have so many things on my mind. Very demanding, being the dean you know.'

'I'm sure.'

The dean tried standing with one foot off the scales. 'It's odd, isn't it, to think that I perform sex exactly the same way as all other men?'

His wife started towelling herself. 'What are you going to do about that vice-chancellor's job?'

'Ask Frankie to offer it to Lancelot. I don't think she'll mind. Hampton Wick are desperate for anybody.'

'But will Lancelot take it?'

The dean switched on his electric razor. 'There's a good chance. He's very fond of Frankie. In fact, he's the only person at St Swithin's she can twist round her little finger. That he is himself an utterly amoral person – not so much permissive as actually stimulative – should recommend him for running a sexual cesspool like that.'

'But will he take it when he hears you've already turned it down?'

The dean laughed. 'He won't hear anything of the kind. Frankie's no fool.' He gave a crafty look. 'And neither am I, dear, eh?'

'Well, what are we going to do about Muriel?'

'Oh God. Let me turn to that after I've got some bacon and eggs inside me.'

Muriel was at that moment breakfasting off a bar of nut chocolate, alone in the St Swithin's library, in front of her on the table an open copy of *Diagnostic Procedures in Clinical Practice*, of which she had not read a word. She sat for some time staring blankly ahead, her long fingers playing with the remains of the chocolate packet. Then she abruptly swept them up and dropped them in the wastepaper basket, snapped shut the book, tucked it under her arm and strode out. She had to find someone to talk to.

It was another sunny morning, and Tulip Twyson was coming briskly through the gate from the main road, notebooks in hand and blonde hair streaming behind. As Muriel hurried towards her across the courtyard, Tulip stopped dead.

'Muriel! What's the matter, love? You look as though you'd seen a ghost. Of one of your own patients, too.'

'You remember what I told you yesterday? About how I was worried? Well –'

'Oh, dear! You mean, you really are preggers?'

Muriel nodded glumly. 'It's for sure. I took a specimen up to the path lab for old Winterflood to test.'

'Perhaps he just made a mistake? He's getting shaky enough these days.'

'I thought of that. I got him to repeat the test, there and then, under my own eyes. I watched his every move. Taking the urine from the specimen bottle – which had my name on. Putting a drop on the black slide. Adding two drops of the reagent –'

'No agglutinization?'

She shook her head. 'Nothing. Not a trace.'

'Poor Muriel! That does sound pretty definite, doesn't it? Of course, these immunilogical tests are not one hundred per cent accurate –'

'They're ninety-eight per cent. That's fair enough, isn't it?'

'I'm afraid it does rather seem you've got a bun in the old oven.'

'It's a terrible shock. Apart from anything else, it'll ruin my chances of the gold medal.'

'That little fat-arsed tick Sharpewhistle will win it.'

'It's his bun.'

'I beg your pardon?'

'Edgar Sharpewhistle's. He put it in the oven. After the May ball.'

'No! But Muriel, you must have been stoned out of your mind?'

'I was a bit woozy, I suppose. More than a bit, possibly. But I admire Edgar, you know. Very much.'

'Of course, I'm sure he's very charming and delightfully entertaining when you get him close to,' Tulip said quickly.

'In fact, I'm going to marry him.'

'Isn't that taking pregnancy rather too seriously altogether?'

'I'm in love with him.'

'Now you're being silly.'

'Well…perhaps I shall grow to love him afterwards. They say it happens.'

'Listen, Muriel, you're hardly the first girl to get herself in pod when she was laid after a party. If they all married the fellers, they'd be doing nobody any good except the divorce lawyers. I know as well as anybody – when you're pissed, anything in trousers looks lovely.'

Muriel looked at her imploringly. 'Then what should I do?'

'Gynae out-patients is at nine.'

She hesitated. 'Do you know, Tulip, I deliberately sought you out this morning. I suppose because I knew subconsciously that you'd persuade me to change my mind. And so take half the responsibility for it. I could never have decided on an abortion all on my own. I relied on you to lead me astray. I'm sorry.'

'A little human failing we see every day, isn't it, love? You should never ask for advice unless you're certain it's really going to be unnecessary.'

'I suppose I'd better tell…the father.'

'I'd say he had a certain interest.'

Muriel looked at her watch. It was just after nine o'clock. She knew her studious fiancé would be in the hospital somewhere. He generally liked to spend an hour before ward-rounds in the pathology museum, looking at the bottles. Leaving Tulip, she retraced her steps of the morning before. This time she did not mount the fire-escape, but went through the main entrance of the pathology building into the room occupying its ground floor. This was filled with racks containing glass bottles of white spirit, in which were items which people had brought into St Swithin's and left without. The only living being in the room was Edgar Sharpewhistle, by the window in his short white coat, soulfully gazing at a jar containing a large spleen with purple patches all over it.

'Edgar, I want to talk to you.'

'Oh, hullo…my love.'

'About the baby. I'm going to lose it.'

He put the spleen on the window ledge with a deliberate motion. 'Changed your mind, then?'

'Yes.'

'I don't know if I care for that.'

'What do you mean? When I told you I was pregnant, the first thing you said was, "Let's get you emptied as soon as the clinic's open".'

'It just seems a pity now. As we're getting married.'

'That won't be necessary, of course.'

Sharpewhistle picked up the bottle again and turned it round slowly, looking at it keenly. 'I don't know about that. I asked your folk. I got myself in the right psychological state for marriage. I've given notice at my digs. I've been to a lot of trouble.'

'I'm extremely sorry if you've put yourself out unnecessarily. But it will be less bother in the long run.'

'But I want to marry you, my love. I'm dead set on it, to tell the truth.'

Muriel tapped her foot impatiently. 'Of course you're not. I only got you into my parents' house at all last night by threatening to make a hysterical scene in the middle of the hospital courtyard.'

'I've been thinking it over. Your dad was right. We'd make an exceptional couple, with our intelligence. We'd go far together at St Swithin's. Your father may be a mean old devil, but he'd certainly ease the way.' Sharpewhistle laughed. 'There never was one for nepotism like the dean, that's what everyone says. He's noticeable even in a place riddled with it like St Swithin's.'

Muriel looked at him witheringly. 'If you had any self-respect, you'd rely on your own brains to get ahead. Anyway, why should you need any help at St Swithin's? From my father or from anyone else.'

'That's fair enough. I could stand on my own feet here. But St Swithin's isn't the whole world, you know, despite a lot of people inside seeming to think so. I'm not going to waste my talents away here. Certainly not! I want to spread my wings. And your dad let out last night that he was getting that vice-chancellor's job at Hampton Wick. The students are bright enough there, even if they are a little high-spirited now and then. And an academic career is something I've always thought myself admirably suited to.'

'You're despicable.'

'I don't think that's the way for a girl to address her future husband.'

'I shall never marry you. Please get that into your head here and now.'

'Oh, yes you will. You can't have an abortion without my consent, you know.'

Her eyes flashed. 'Of course I can. The father does not have to sign the form. It's a particularly valuable principle under the Act.'

'Yes, but people will think it funny, won't they, when I let it out you won't marry the father of your child, who's devoted to you –'

'Are you mad? How can two people seriously talk of marriage when they're not even remotely in love?'

'There's countless examples in history, of princes and princesses betrothed in infancy and being as happy as turtle-doves in the end. A couple of our intellect shouldn't have any trouble over a little thing like that. It's only emotional adjustment.'

'You don't seem to consider what it would be like for the child, growing up in an atmosphere like that.'

'Well, it couldn't be worse off than not being born at all, could it?'

She bit her lip. This seemed unanswerable. 'I think I'd prefer to die myself.'

'Rather be dead than wed, eh?' Sharpewhistle inspected his spleen again. 'By the way, I saw your dad – our dad – as I came into the hospital. I'm invited to dinner tonight. Your place, seven-thirty sharp. He wanted to tell you, but it seems you left home this morning a little on the early side. Funny, isn't it, to think that from next Monday you and I'll be sleeping in the same bed every night for the rest of our lives.'

'If you must know, Edgar, that is a prospect which fills me with horror, if not outright alarm.'

'You didn't seem to mind last time.'

'You aren't much good at it.'

'How do you know? Who've you got to compare me with?'

She bit her lip again. This seemed unanswerable, too.

'See you at lunch in the refectory, then?'

'Lunch? No, I'm not having any today. I'm too busy. I've work to do at home.'

'Suit yourself.' He put the spleen back on its shelf. 'I'm glad the old folk asked me tonight. I've a couple of sticky cases I'd like to thrash out with the dean.'

11

The morning storm was over as suddenly as it had started. The black clouds hurried to continue their business eastwards, and there was the English countryside at its most beautiful, smiling at Sir Lancelot Spratt through remorseful tears. He looked at his half-hunter, seeing it was just on ten o'clock. He stepped from the shelter of an elm, where he had been sombrely calculating the statistics of being struck by lightning. He shook himself, like a dog out of a pond. He flicked his deerstalker, producing a cloud of drops. He was wet all through, right down to his fruit-gums.

The treacherous brightness earlier had conned him into leaving his waterproof at the Pike and Eel Inn, where he had spent the night. He had a bleeding lobe to his right ear, which he had caught with his dry fly. He had caught also that morning two trees, half-a-dozen bushes, a barbed-wire fence and the district nurse cycling across the bridge by the seat of her knickers. Of fish, he had only two miserable brown trout – which he supposed would do for Bonaccord's pot – which had surrendered with such shaming lack of fight he excused them as having marked suicidal tendencies.

Sir Lancelot was fond of quoting *The Compleat Angler*, that fly-fishing was a rest to the mind, a cheerer of the spirits, a diverter of sadness, a calmer of unquiet thoughts, a moderator of passions, a procurer of contentedness that begat habits of peace or patience in those that professed and practised it. Or less elaborately, the notice he had once seen up in a riverside pub –

If you want to be happy for a day, get drunk. If you want to be happy for a week, get married. But if you want to be happy for life, take up fishing.

As he now squelched along the grassy river bank, he had to admit that morning had brought his spirits as little cheer, his thoughts as little calmness, as driving down Piccadilly in the rush-hour.

He stopped as he reached the reed-fringed edge of Frying-Pan Pool. Here the river tumbled under a bridge of russet brick which stood beside a handful of weather-beaten cottages, then expanded to a swift-flowing sheet between the rich green water meadows. It was not so exciting as Carrot's Pool further downstream, believed to hold a trout comparable with the Loch Ness Monster, and probably equally mythical. But there was a plump one or two Sir Lancelot had seen from the bridge, which he felt he had a bone to pick with. He detached the dry-fly from the cork handle of his rod, then with the precision and delicacy of movement which so graced the operating theatre, cast it as lightly as falling thistledown on the water. He gave a deep sigh. When he was fishing, his troubles usually fled like vampires at daybreak, but that morning Miss MacNish and her horrible cats were unbudgeable from his mind. She would have to go, bag, cats and baggage. But he could never find so superb nor devoted a cook, and the prospect of breaking another housekeeper to his ways appalled him. Yet no employer, even in such democratic days, could pass uncensured a dish of tripe and onions thrown at him. Where he would get her replacement was another problem, which Sir Lancelot decided to ponder on later. No man could think with a clear head when his shoes were half-full of rainwater.

'Any luck?'

Sir Lancelot turned. A young man of about seventeen in a white helmet was grinning at him from a scooter stopped on the bridge.

'Luck!' he muttered. On that river, in the finest angling country of England, if not of the world! Where well-bred trout were caught with enormous skill in an atmosphere of dry-flies, well-cut tweeds and clipped accents. 'There is little luck concerned with the operation, I'm afraid,' he called back.

'What you using? Worms?'

Sir Lancelot choked. It was a word never mentioned among the members of his fishing club. There was one half-forgotten dreadful scandal about a member – a clerical one, at that – who had been unmasked on some quiet reach removing his regulation dry-fly and substituting a juicy maggot. 'I am using toasted cheese.'

'Go on? Are they biting today?'

'They do not bite,' said Sir Lancelot icily. 'They suck.'

He cast his line again, scowling fiercely enough to send every fish hurrying in terror up the river. Why, he wondered, had a man's traditional privacy at prayer or fishing to be violated by itinerant ignoramuses in hard hats?

'Why don't you sit down to it? You wouldn't get so tired then, would you?'

'I regret that I suffer from a painful condition of the posterior.'

'Oh, got the Farmer Giles, have you?' asked the onlooker knowingly. 'I wouldn't mind having a go with that rod of yours.'

'Doubtless.'

'Doctor – ?'

Sir Lancelot spun round. From the cottage next to the bridge appeared Pilcher the river-keeper, a little man with a pipe who Sir Lancelot felt closely resembled Popeye the Sailor. But Pilcher loved all the fish as his children, and had river-water rather than blood in his veins. 'Telephone call for you, Doctor. Urgent. From London.'

Sir Lancelot cursed. 'Who is it?'

'Don't know, Doctor. The wife took it.'

Sir Lancelot knew he had an intense suspicion of telephones. He carefully rested his rod in the fork of a small tree. Wiping his hands on his red-spotted handkerchief, he tramped into the cottage parlour and picked up the instrument.

'Spratt here.'

'Lancelot dear, you *do* sound in a mood.'

'Who the hell's that?'

'Frankie.'

Sir Lancelot bit his lip. 'I have had a very trying morning. Among other things being half-drowned in a storm.'

'Yes, it's just blowing up over London now. Miss MacNish gave me this telephone number. I've invited myself to dinner tonight. Seven-thirty all right?'

Sir Lancelot grunted.

'I heard you'd be back by lunchtime, and of course I'd love to taste some of her wonderful cooking again.'

'As you know, Frankie, I am delighted to see you at any time.'

'Well, you don't sound as if you'd particularly care to at the moment. But what I've got to say when we meet will put you in a much better mood. I'm sure of that. It's something extremely important, but an official matter, so I can't mention it over the phone. See you this evening.'

He put down the telephone. He went through the cottage door. He crossed the front garden and the road leading to the bridge. He made down towards the bank of Frying-Pan Pool. He stopped dead, quivering all over.

'You! Put that valuable rod down this instant.'

The youth from the scooter, still in his white helmet, looked round with a grin. 'You're right. It's more difficult than it looks.'

Sir Lancelot advanced, grabbing the cork rod handle. 'What the hell do you mean, poaching anyway?'

'I didn't think you'd mind.'

'I do mind. Enormously.' Sir Lancelot put his free hand over his eyes. 'Please go,' he said weakly. 'Be on your way, on your contraption. Had I the mind to, I could have you prosecuted, and the local bench would undoubtedly view your conduct with the greatest severity. You would probably have to go to prison for several months. As it happens, I have had far too much to put up with this morning already. And I must anyway be off home. Leave an old man in peace. Please. My dear chap.'

'Okay, dad.' The youth gave another grin. Sir Lancelot watched him in silence as he mounted his scooter and with an explosion of the engine disappeared. He gave a weary sigh and started to reel in his line from the swirling waters.

'The bloody fool's jammed my fly into some underwater weeds,' he growled. 'Or a submerged log, by the feel of it.'

He stopped. His mouth fell open. The line of its own accord started to swim about.

'Pilcher!'

The keeper's head appeared over the bridge.

'Pilcher! I seem to have got into something like a baby seal.'

'Christ!'

An enormous fish leapt into the air then shot powerfully across the pool.

'Pilcher!' Sir Lancelot's fishing-line screamed out. 'Don't stand there, man! Come and help me.' Pipe still in mouth, the keeper scrambled down the bank. 'Net, man, net!' shouted Sir Lancelot, as though demanding the artery forceps in a hurry.

'Your net won't be big enough, sir.'

'Then jump in the water and carry him out with your bare hands.'

'Can't swim, Doctor.'

'My God, Pilcher, if I lose this fish up the river you'll follow it, with a couple of bricks round your neck.'

The battle started. The monster fish produced every trick from several million years' evolution to detach itself from Sir Lancelot. The huntsman used every trick from the comparatively few years he had evolved from his prey to keep him on. Both were fighting in their own element – one with the better brain, but the other with the better instincts. For half an hour the fight continued without slackening, as the fish reared and plunged, buried itself under blankets of weed, sprang into the air, wound itself round the bridge, shot abruptly in the direction of the sea or turned and charged Sir Lancelot's boots as he crashed anxiously through the weeds, soaking up to his thighs, spirits rising and falling like the temperature-chart of some terrible fever. At last the great fish surrendered. It rolled wearily on its handsome back, it allowed itself to be reeled unresistingly towards the bank, where Pilcher had fetched a bigger net and was jumping up and down uttering anguished cries of unheard advice.

'My God,' muttered Sir Lancelot, as the trout made its fatal transition from water to grass. 'Now I know how Ahab felt on sighting Moby Dick.'

'Eight pounds, sir,' exclaimed Pilcher wonderingly.

'Oh, more than that. Ten at least. Possibly fifteen.'

'Biggest in my memory of the river, Doctor.'

'And in the memory of your grandfather, too, I'd imagine.'

'How'd you catch him, sir?'

'Why, I – ' Sir Lancelot paused. He stroked his beard. 'When I came back from the telephone I'd my eye on him, moving over at the far side of the bridge. I shot a low cast under the arch.'

Pitcher chewed his pipe thoughtfully. 'Long cast.'

'Very.'

'Difficult, too. Into the wind.'

'Pitcher, I have had a good many years' experience at this sport, you know.'

'I'd say it was a cast which would win a championship record for distance.'

'Perhaps it was a little nearer than it looks.' Sir Lancelot was aware that Pilcher knew more about angling than he about surgery.

'Funny how you managed to miss hooking those overhanging willows, Doctor.'

'Skill, Pilcher, sheer skill. Here – buy yourself a bottle of scotch to celebrate.'

'Thank you, Doctor. Well, this trout'll make you a fine dinner.'

'Good God, I'm not going to eat it. I'm going to tie it to a board and take it back to London to be stuffed. Then you may hang it in a glass case in the club's rod-room. And all the other fishermen can come and look at it. By God, I can just see the old major and the vicar now, absolutely sick with envy.'

'I still don't see how you could notice it moving behind the bridge. Not from here, Doctor.'

'Pilcher, buy yourself a second bottle of scotch.'

'Thank you, Doctor,'

'No point in celebrating by halves. Take this – buy a case.'

'Thank you, sir,

'Now I must be off to London. I'll have to drive like stink as it is.'

'But you're wet through, Doctor.'

Sir Lancelot at last gave a broad grin. 'Am I? To tell you the truth, I really don't notice it.'

12

The storm reached London about noon. It was still raining about an hour later, as Muriel hurried out of No 2 Lazar Row, where she had slipped unobserved to fetch her white belted mackintosh. Her way along the main road brought her past the gates of St Swithin's itself, where she looked anxiously for Sharpewhistle. But he was a man of industrious and regular habits, who would be working in the wards until his refectory lunch. Stepping along briskly, staring straight ahead, she went into the underground station and bought a ticket for Piccadilly Circus.

She emerged from the tube by the Shaftesbury Avenue entrance, looking anxiously at her watch. Almost one fifteen. A girl of Muriel's conscientious mind always liked to be on time. It was still spitting with rain as she hurried into the tawdry criss-cross of narrow Soho Streets. The pub was on a corner, next to a pornographic bookshop and an open doorway with the invitation *Young French Model Walk Up* – probably not French, nor young and certainly not a model, she reflected. She hesitated. It would be the public bar. She pushed open the door and saw she had guessed right.

'Hello, Muriel. Do you mind mixing with the peasants?'

'No, of course not...'

'They tend to look askance at my appearance in the saloon bar. Besides, it's cheaper here. What'll you have?'

'What are you drinking yourself?'

'Tomato juice, as usual.'

'I'll have a double whisky.'

'Well! That's depraved for a sober and studious girl like you, isn't it?'

'I need it. I've something difficult to tell you. Something awful.'

He ordered the drink. He was a man of her own age, pale, fashionably covered with drooping hair, thin, taller than she. Though dressed in a pair of faded, patched jeans, a white round-necked undervest, and a worn quilted green anorak he presented a refreshingly hygienic appearance, as though himself and his underclothes were well-scrubbed daily – as they were.

'What's the awful news, Muriel? You've fallen in love with somebody else?'

'Well...no. But...oh, Andy! I can hardly tell you. I'm getting married to somebody else.'

'That might lead to our seeing rather less of each other.'

'It's happening on Monday.'

'That certainly shows enthusiasm for the married state on your part.'

'It's got to be done as soon as possible. You see, I'm having a baby. There, I've got it all out, right at the start,' She picked up her glass and swilled the whisky at a gulp.

'Have another.'

'Thank you.'

'How did it happen?'

'It was after a dance. One of the students. The stupid thing is, it was all over in a flash... I really *did* believe it went on for rather longer. I didn't enjoy it. Not at all. It's beyond me how everyone all over the world seems to get so excited about it.'

He sipped his tomato juice. 'Poor, poor Muriel.'

'Oh, Andy! I knew you'd say something like that.' She smiled her gratitude. 'That's why I just had to see you today. I could have just left you in ignorance, couldn't I? I could easily have avoided ever meeting you again.'

'But I've nothing but compassion and sympathy for you, Muriel. I don't see why I should modify my philosophy of life just because something painful affects me so personally.'

She dropped her eyes, leaving her second drink untouched. 'You're an angel. A saint.'

'I hope not – you've got to be far too aggressive and bossy and generally interfering to be a saint. It's simply that I believe in gentleness and purity in life. That's all.'

'It's a lovely outlook.'

'It's a depressing one. Everyone who's tried it from Our Lord onwards has come to a sticky end.'

'Perhaps that was our trouble – you and me. We were too pure.'

'Oh, purity's dead kinky these days.'

'I mean, if we'd *done* it, like everyone else…' She looked at him imploringly. 'Why didn't we get married, Andy, months ago?'

'It would have wrecked your career.'

'Why should it have done? Nearly all the girls at St Swithin's are married.'

'Yes, but to respectable students and wage-earners, not to oddments like me. And it would have wrecked your family. I wouldn't have liked the responsibility for that. I don't think your father would entirely approve of my total rejection of society. Nor of your meeting me on a sociology course – as material.'

'I don't care tuppence about my father, or anyone else.'

'Perhaps not now, when you're rather desperate.' Muriel said nothing. 'You're going ahead with the baby?'

She nodded. 'I'd resolved to get rid of it – it wasn't easy, you know, like it always seems in films and novels. But then he said he wanted to go ahead and have it.'

'I suppose I can only say I hope you'll be very happy.'

'Oh, Andy, thank you.' She suddenly started to cry loudly. Andy clasped her tightly. The other drinkers pointedly tried to pretend nothing abnormal was happening. Couples got up to all manner of things in pubs these days. 'But what am I going to *do*?' she implored.

'You haven't left yourself much room to manoeuvre, dear, I must say.'

'But I don't love him. Not a bit. That business after the ball…it meant no more than kissing someone in the dark. I know all the other girls seem to go about it the same way, but I've learnt my lesson, I don't mind admitting.'

'What's he like?'

'Oh…about five feet tall, tubby, with small feet and a large head.'

'Sounds charming.'

They fell silent. She looked up at him, dabbing her cheeks with a handkerchief from her large handbag. 'So it's goodbye, Andy. It must have upset you tremendously. I'm sorry. But I had to tell you about it. It was only right and fair, wasn't it? Besides, it's made me feel so much better, just talking to you like this.'

'No, it isn't goodbye. I don't agree at all.'

She smiled wanly. 'We can hardly ask you to the wedding.'

'Today's Tuesday. So there's almost a week for something to happen. Of course, there's always the chance he may walk under a bus, or at least see reason.'

'He's far too canny for either, I think.'

'Let me think up something.'

'What?'

Andy shrugged his thin shoulders. 'I don't know but can I get in touch with you tomorrow?'

'Ring the phone box in the students' common-room at twelve-thirty. I'll be waiting. And I'll make sure he's somewhere else.'

'Don't you want the whisky?'

'No, not really. I've work to do this afternoon. Sorry I let you in for buying it.'

'Money is meaningless when you live on faith, hope and charity.' They went outside. The rain had stopped and the sun had come through, raising steam from the glistening pavements and the roofs of the crawling traffic. 'Look at Nature's frugal housekeeping,' Andy observed. 'What the skies send down they take back again in due course. As it was and ever shall be. The world doesn't change, you know. No more than a wheel changes, going faster and faster along a bumpy track. Tell me, your father the revered dean of St Swithin's. Is he a healthy man?'

'He seems to be. He's been a bit depressed recently, that's all.'

'I mean his heart is strong?'

'Yes. He had a test the other week.'

'He wouldn't succumb to a sudden shock?'

'He seems proof against them, poor man.'

'Good. I'll telephone you tomorrow, my love. Without fail.'

He gave her a pure kiss, and she hurried back to the hospital.

13

Sir Lancelot Spratt was at that moment switching off the engine of his Rolls in his garage across the road from No 3 Lazar Row. The troubles left behind him hadn't crossed his mind since seizing his fishing rod back that morning on the bank of frying-pan pool. Only as he reached the front door, reverently bearing the huge trout on a length of plank, did he wince at the prospect of mollifying an infuriated housekeeper. She would doubtless be luxuriating in a fit of the sulks, if he knew her – skilfully mixing an impression of offendedness and servility, perhaps with a hint of high-minded forgiveness, which would be insufferable. He unlatched the door and stood in the hall. Silence. It occurred to him suddenly that she might have fled. That would be even worse – having to get his own lunch, and Frankie inviting herself for dinner as well. But there were more important things to be decided first.

Sir Lancelot crossed the hall and pushed open a door into the small kitchen. He opened a cupboard and took out a hefty spring-balance. Heart pounding, he set it on the table, adjusted the pointer to zero, and gently laid the fish on the pan. He caught his breath as the needle spun round. Eight pounds two ounces. He touched the pan with his finger, but withdrew it guiltily. Eight pounds two was good enough. Almost the national record for a rainbow trout. He glowed as he already visualized it in its glass case, lacquered and glass-eyed, a brass plate below proclaiming *Caught by Sir Lancelot Sprats FRCS*, to be admired and envied in the rod-room not only by the major and the vicar but generations of fishermen yet unborn.

He heard the quiet tinkle of cutlery in the next room. He stiffened his shoulders. He had better face her.

Miss MacNish was in the dining-room taking the cover from a plate of cold ham and tongue, beside it a salad of lettuce, tomatoes and sliced hard-boiled eggs. She dropped her eyes remorsefully. 'As I thought you might be late, Sir Lancelot, I put out something cold. I hope that will be adequate?'

'It looks most inviting, Miss MacNish.'

She started to toss the salad. 'Did you pass a comfortable night, Sir Lancelot?'

'Perfectly comfortable, Miss MacNish. An outing is always the more enjoyable for being unexpected.'

'I'm very glad, Sir Lancelot.'

'Thank you, Miss MacNish.'

He sat down, suddenly realizing he was hungry. She went on with the salad, unseeingly.

'Oh, Sir Lancelot – !'

'Yes, Miss MacNish?'

'I spoke hastily last night, Sir Lancelot.'

He looked at her with a compassionate but slightly pained expression, like the Recording Angel permitting a fresh start. 'I think we had best overlook it, Miss MacNish.'

'The tripe, Sir Lancelot. It all went to waste.'

'I don't think that need embarrass the household exchequer.'

'After you left, I... I could have cut my hand off, Sir Lancelot.'

'Nor do I think such radical surgery called for, Miss MacNish.'

He started on the cold ham. He wished she would stop mucking about with the salad and give him some. 'It was very difficult about my cats, Sir Lancelot.' He raised an eyebrow, hoping for the moment she had evicted them, or dropped them in a sack into the Thames. 'You see, I have so little companionship... I've no family left in the world... I never married.'

'I'm sure, Miss MacNish, the last was not for want of asking.'

'Oh, Sir Lancelot –' To his horror he saw a tear splash into the salad, hitting a hard-boiled egg. 'I nearly left you last night.'

'Please feel free to resign at any time that you wish, of course. Though I make no secret that your absence would cause me considerable distress.'

'But it's unthinkable! I should never be happy away from you, Sir

Lancelot.' She stirred the salad more vigorously still. He noticed one of the eggs was disintegrating. 'I've grown so used to you, Sir Lancelot.'

'And perhaps I to you, Miss MacNish.'

'I'm really...really very fond of you, Sir Lancelot.'

'Naturally, I have over the years developed an attachment to yourself Miss MacNish. Living in close quarters, that is inescapable. Do you think I could have a little salad?' Women were prey to emotional disturbances at her particular time in life, he thought. It was best to humour her. 'Perhaps you and I *should* see a little more of each other. It's quite abnormal that we should be so near and yet so far, if you follow me. I don't see why we shouldn't be intimate, do you, Miss MacNish?'

'Oh, Sir Lancelot!' Turning pink, she spooned some greenery on to his plate.

He was pleased to see her touched by his kindness. 'Now if you'll excuse me, I have a lot of work to get through before our guest arrives this evening. I know Dr Humble appreciates your cooking – though not nearly so much, I'm sure, as I myself.'

She hurried from the room in delighted confusion. 'A plump and pleasing person,' he quoted absently. He drew from his inside pocket the dean's obituary. He read it again carefully as he ate everything in sight – the ham, the cold apple pie, the chunk of Stilton, the dish of walnuts pickled by Miss MacNish herself. He uncapped his fountain-pen to make an alteration. *Lychfield's later years were undeniably of some sadness, and sometimes of some embarrassment, to his family and friends, after he was abruptly seized with a madness involving bizarre hallucinations.* Sir Lancelot looked up. He wrinkled his nose, He began uncontrollably to tremble. Slowly, he forced himself to cast his eyes round the room. There was one about somewhere.

He laid down the pen. He clasped his hands, turning the knuckles white. He could not do without Miss MacNish. She and her vermin were hopelessly inseparable. So he must make the superhuman effort of tolerating them. 'Tenderness,' he muttered. 'Like a baby.' He started violently. There was Kensington, the lean grey one. It was sitting on the ledge of the open window, washing itself.

'Pussy-wussy,' said Sir Lancelot.

Kensington leapt from the window and rubbed itself against his hairy tweed trouser-leg, purring loudly.

He gingerly reached down a hand. 'What a nice little baby you are! What a bonnie child! Diddums, then? Come to daddy, there's a dear ickle fing.'

He suddenly scooped it up. He sat with it on his knee, stroking it vigorously. A broad smile broke across his troubled features. 'I've managed it! All done by transference. By God, that feller Bonaccord can't be so damn stupid as he looks. Nice baby! Pretty puss!' He went on stroking it delightedly. It struck him the animal was more docile than usual – most fortunate for such a delicate experiment. He supposed it had recently been fed. It had settled comfortably in his lap, eyes closed, still purring contentedly. Then Sir Lancelot noticed a flake of pinkish, raw fish caught in the fur of its back.

Kensington went flying. He pulled open the door of the kitchen. Chelsea, the black one, looked up in surprise. It was perched on the scales, with some fish-bones, some fins and the head. It leapt for cover under the sink, but Sir Lancelot was too quick. He grabbed the cat by the tail and held it up. The door from the hall opened. Miss MacNish stood on the threshold.

'My poor Chelsea!'

He dropped it squawking to the floor. 'Your bloody cats have eaten my fish.'

She glanced at the remains on the scales. 'In that case, I am extremely sorry, Sir Lancelot. I am quite prepared to reimburse you the cost from my wages.'

'Cost! Do you realize, woman, that fish was entirely irreplaceable? Why, those cats might just as well have finished eating the Mona Lisa.'

'I'm afraid they were rather hungry, Sir Lancelot. They wouldn't look at the new sort of cat-food I tried on them this morning.'

'I don't care if they were starving to death –'

'You were very cruel, holding Chelsea up like that. It couldn't have been any good for its tail-joints at all.'

Sir Lancelot said something which even at that moment surprised him. 'You're sacked.'

She stared at him. 'How can you say that?'

'Why shouldn't I? When the happiness of a lifetime has been consumed by your cats.'

'One moment you are making indecent suggestions to me –'

'What!'

'You call yourself "an English gentleman". Well, the whole world knows what that means. An English barefaced hypocrite. Don't you imagine I haven't noticed the hungry way you've been looking at me –'

'How do you expect me to look, when I'm waiting for my blasted dinner?'

'Then just a moment ago, you suggested intimacy.'

'Good God. You must be mad. Absolutely mad. Like the dean. I'd be obliged if you kept strictly to your flat until you leave at the end of the month.'

'I shall be leaving today, thank you. You can hardly expect me to spend another night under the same roof as a dirty-minded old man, can you? Though in my book, cruelty towards human beings is not nearly so revolting as cruelty to poor dumb animals who can't stand up for themselves. Come, you poor dears...'

She gathered both cats from the floor. She left the room. Sir Lancelot stood gazing at the remains on the scales. Slowly, he shook his head. 'The enormous skill I brought to that catch,' he muttered brokenly. 'That superb cast, under the bridge...' He produced his handkerchief and blew his nose loudly. He went out to the sitting-room, collapsing into his chair, staring ahead blankly. Half an hour went by, before he heard Miss MacNish thumping downstairs with her cases. He looked through the window. She was clutching a brown wicker basket which moved of its own accord. He supposed she had telephoned for a taxi. He certainly wasn't going to offer her a lift to King's Cross. The door slammed violently behind her. He shut his eyes. He hoped the cats would enjoy the bracing fish-scented atmosphere of Aberdeen.

14

When the front door of No 3 slammed after Miss MacNish, the dean in No 2 winced as his silver running cups rattled once again in their glass case. 'I do wish the fellow would learn to leave his house in a civilized manner,' he muttered irritably. 'You'd imagine that every time he went out he was being blasted off to the moon.'

He turned back to the sitting-room sofa, on which lay Dr Bonaccord with a bare midriff.

'So it's nothing serious?' asked the psychiatrist anxiously.

'I don't think so. The history hardly suggests a peptic ulcer, nor anything particularly definite at all. I am certainly not anxious to submit you to barium meal screening, or anything quite so uncomfortable at this stage. We'll wait and see. Drop in again in a fortnight.'

Dr Bonaccord sat up, tucking a mauve-striped shirt into his trousers. 'Then what's the cause of the pain?'

'As far as one can pinpoint a cause for these things in every case, I would say irregular and unsuitably cooked meals.'

'The bachelor's perennial problem?'

'It would seem so. Even in these days of instant pre-cooked everything. Couldn't you employ someone to do for you?'

'They're not easy to come by. I've cast my eyes round, but without much success.'

The dean gave a laugh. 'Well, I can only suggest you take a wife, Bonaccord.'

'That treatment might be a little radical. I'm too set in my ways.'

'Oh, come. You're a young man. Not like me. I'm well into middle age.

I'm finished. All passion spent. A burnt-out roman candle. Or perhaps only a squib?'

Dr Bonaccord at once looked interested. 'How long have you suffered from those sort of feelings?'

'About six months. Since my son George got married.'

'Perhaps you'd care to talk to me about them?'

'Well…now you mention it…'

'Why not make yourself comfortable? Lie down.' A little shamefacedly, the dean took his patient's place on the sofa. Dr Bonaccord brought up a chair at his head. 'What's the main trouble?'

'That I have nothing whatever left to aim for in life. Nothing! All that lies before me is a well-tarmacked dead straight motorway leading to the grave.'

'Ah! The death wish.'

The dean looked up irritably. 'I thought you psycho fellows had rather dropped that concept?'

'A lot of Freud's teaching has become unfashionable, of course. And personally, I simply don't believe that *all* adult activities are sublimations of the sexual drive. Just because my secretary's fond of bananas, for instance, doesn't mean to say she's an obsessional fellatrice.'

The dean looked rather shocked. 'She…er, seems a perfectly healthy young woman. I mean, one couldn't imagine her…that is…'

'But there's something in the death wish. It has been brought across to us very strongly by highly articulate men of genius. It's the mainspring of Maugham's *Of Human Bondage*, you know. There was Edgar Allan Poe, of course, absolutely obsessed by it. And John Keats! Do you know what he wrote to Fanny Brawne? "I have two luxuries to brood over in my walks, your loveliness and the hour of my death. O that I could have possession of them both in the same minute." He wanted to do her and drop dead at the same time. You couldn't be more explicit, could you?'

'But what's all this got to do with me?' the dean asked somewhat irritably.

'I was coming to that.' The psychiatrist looked down at him thoughtfully, rubbing his pudgy hands together. 'You are obsessed with the idea of your inevitable dissolution. Right?'

'Well…quite obviously one's view changes about such things. Before thirty, you take for granted that your span on earth is limitless. Afterwards, you're inclined to see your days are numbered. That's why the young drive cars so badly. I can't imagine there's anything pathological in that.'

'*Of course* our outlook changes. "At eighteen our convictions are hills from which we look; at forty-five they are caves in which we hide." Eh? That was by Scott Fitzgerald, an alcoholic psychopath. What you need, dean, is something to shake you up. To give you a completely new interest. To change your life entirely, overnight.'

'Funny you should say that. In professional confidence, I was offered a new job only yesterday. But I turned it down. Funked it, I suppose. It isn't easy adapting yourself at my age, you know.'

'Not when you're suffering from the male menopause.'

'Now you're being disgusting.'

'But you can't ignore your menopause, dean,' Dr Bonaccord went on earnestly. 'It's a purely physical condition, which Strauss described rather touchingly in *Psychiatry in the Modern World* – "the smouldering fire of the endocrines in which from time to time certain embers flare up, emit sparks and subside into cold ashes".'

'I suppose those sparks might possibly be fun,' observed the dean unhappily.

'Life loses its savour, its freshness, its excitement, doesn't it?' The dean nodded. 'Look at you – tense, anxious, forever driving yourself onward, a perfectionist, ambitious, always keen to shine above your fellows, over-conscientious, avid for responsibility, taut, tired, exhausted.'

'Exactly.' The dean looked gratified with this diagnosis.

'And your sexual activity not a patch on what it was?'

'Only on special occasions.'

'It's useless my telling you to relax, to go on a cruise, to take a holiday. That's only a layman's way of looking at the problem. With nothing to occupy your restless mind you'd get worse. Even suicidal. You need this fundamental new interest in life, that's all.'

'But what?'

'There's the rub. Only you can answer that. You know, it is precisely this situation which makes a fair number of men of your age go off with much younger women.'

'Oh, I don't think Josephine would allow me to do that, for one moment.'

Dr Bonaccord looked at his watch. 'I must be going, I'm afraid. I have another appointment in a few minutes.'

The dean sat up. 'I've a good deal of worry, possibly aggravating my condition at this moment. My daughter Muriel, you know. Very trying.'

'I'm afraid tension is normal in any family. Quite understandable, when you remember that with the Oedipus situation basically the son wants to castrate the father and sleep with the mother. Daughters have the Electra complex, of course, which is the same thing the other way round.'

'Perhaps I should take up golf?' the dean suggested hopefully. 'At least it would keep me fit. We doctors should look after ourselves, I suppose. We die just like our patients, from exactly the same diseases.'

Dr Bonaccord smiled. 'A little *infra dig*, you feel? Yet even the nicest patients enjoy an inward glow of satisfaction, or perhaps of triumph, when they hear their doctor has predeceased them. You know, dean, human beings are really the most peculiar objects.'

15

Sir Lancelot looked at his watch. His afternoon appointment would be in a few minutes. He rose from the chair, where he had remained since Miss MacNish quit No 3. He could not face entering the kitchen, with evidence of the awful crime still unburied. He went into the hall, where he had dropped his fishing-bag, and removing two miserable trout wrapped them in a sheet from that morning's *Times*. He opened the front door and stepped out. Whatever its tragedies, life still had to go on.

This occasion he was too dispirited to conceal his visiting No 1. Besides, he had the obvious excuse of bringing a neighbourly gift of fish. But when Mrs Tennant opened the door, she jumped back with a gasp.

'I had an appointment.' Sir Lancelot looked surprised. 'Weren't you expecting me?'

'Well, it was a bit of a surpr – Yes, of course we were expecting you, Sir Lancelot. Dr Bonaccord has just got in. Would you care to go upstairs?'

'Thank you.' Why on earth is the young woman staring at me like that? he wondered. She looks as though I was forcing my way in to pinch the silver. But I suppose living in sin must make one somewhat anxious. Her husband might quite easily knock on the door one day with a loaded revolver. *That* would liven up the street a bit.

Still carrying his fish, Sir Lancelot mounted to the first-floor study. The door was open, but the psychiatrist was absent. Sir Lancelot went inside, idly inspecting a pair of Leonardo prints attached to the walls, Dr Bonaccord bounced in, pinker than ever and breathless.

'So sorry, Lancelot. Quite frankly, I wasn't entirely expecting you at this moment.'

'I had arranged to appear at this particular time,' Sir Lancelot told him bleakly.

'Yes, but I thought you might have had second thoughts.'

'Why should I?'

'No, of course not… You like my Leonardos? That's *Madonna and Child with St Anne*. The original is in the Louvre, I expect you can see the vulture.'

'Vulture? What vulture?'

'Slightly subliminal, I suppose, but discernible in the folds of the dress. Haven't you read Freud's book on Leonardo? About the dream Leonardo had as a baby, when a vulture put its tail in his mouth and fluttered it? That meant Leonardo was a homosexual, of course.'

'Oh, of course.'

'The vulture's tail cannot possibly signify anything but the penis.'

'Naturally.'

'Indeed, the word *coda* or tail is used by the Italians to mean the male organ. And the Egyptian goddess Mut, which has the head of a vulture, is equipped not only with female breasts but an erect phallus. Very significant, that.'

'Very.' This man's as nutty as a vegetarian's cutlet, thought Sir Lancelot.

'Leonardo used to dream of flying, you know. So he invented the aeroplane.'

'I frequently dream that I am flying myself.'

Dr Bonaccord smiled. 'According to Freud, that means you have a longing to be capable of sexual performance.' Sir Lancelot made a suppressed choking noise, 'But don't worry, a large percentage of all dreams are set in some form of transport. Just reflect a moment, and I think you'll agree.'

'I dream most often that I am hammering outsized nails into a block of ebony.'

'Oh, dear,' said the psychiatrist, suddenly looking concerned.

'I have however managed to cure myself of that cat thing.'

'Good. I'm delighted.'

'Or rather the condition has to some extent cured itself.' He gave a small shudder. 'Odd. I had the feeling again, very slightly. Pure imagination, of course. You'd understand such matters. I'm glad I'm a surgeon, cutting out things I can see. I'd be no good trying to cure shadows.' He jumped. 'What's that?' he cried in alarm. 'A soft padding noise?'

'I didn't hear anything. Perhaps it's my secretary moving about downstairs.'

Sir Lancelot wiped his face with the red and white handkerchief. 'Possibly. You know, she looked at me extremely strangely when I arrived. There is nothing particularly noticeably odd about me, is there?'

Dr Bonaccord moved towards the study door. 'Not in the slightest. She may have had something on her mind.'

'H'm. Her husband's out in Sydney, I believe?' he went on, following this train of thought.

'Yes.' The psychiatrist was making for the stairs, seeming unenthusiastic about the conversation.

'Forgive my mentioning it – I gather there's some estrangement between them – but I believe I actually met him. At a party, when I was lecturing out there last winter.'

'Oh, I'm sure you didn't.'

'But why not? Sydney is not such a huge place. Jim Tennant – young, good-looking fellow, something in shipping.'

'Gisela's husband is elderly, decrepit, a farmer and called Arthur. Or so I gather.'

They reached the foot of the stairs before Sir Lancelot remembered his gift. 'Here's the brace of trout I promised you, Bonaccord. Nothing special, but they'll make a tasty supper.'

'How kind of you! An appropriately luxurious dish, I think, for our new cook to apply her skill to.'

'Oh? You've taken on a cook, have you?'

'Almost for therapeutic reasons. My own efforts have been playing hell with my digestion.'

'I'd be interested to hear how you laid hands on her. As it happens, I'm in the market for one myself.'

'I'd heard of her for some time, actually.'

'You were very wise to grab her while you could.'

'I'm sure I was.'

Sir Lancelot quivered. The kitchen door opened and the ample figure of Miss MacNish appeared in her smart cornflower overall.

'Did you want me, Dr Bonaccord?'

'If it wouldn't disrupt your plans, perhaps we could have these fish for supper?'

'It wouldn't disrupt anything in the slightest, Dr Bonaccord. I am only here to do what you wish, and to make you as comfortable as possible. Would you like them done in a *court bouillon*? Or perhaps grilled in best butter with fresh herbs?'

'I would leave that entirely to you, Miss MacNish.'

'Perhaps with almonds would be more tasty? They're not very large ones. Hardly enough to make a meal.'

'Miss MacNish! What the devil are you up to?'

She stared at Sir Lancelot as though he were some intrusive stranger. 'I am employed here, sir.'

'You are to come home at once.'

'Will that be all, Dr Bonaccord?'

'Thank you, Miss MacNish. All for now.'

'Bonaccord! What do you mean by poaching my cook?'

'But I gathered the good lady was unemployed,' the psychiatrist told him blandly. 'I have in fact for some months had an open invitation for her to work here. But with the most admirable loyalty she has always refused me, until this afternoon.'

'You traitor —'

'Come, Lancelot. I know you may be upset, but after all it's a free country with a free labour market.'

'Shall I show the gentleman to the door, Doctor?'

'Very well, Bonaccord. Very well. Keep her. I hope that you will enjoy the company of her flea-ridden cats.' He glared at Miss MacNish. 'Personally, I should prefer to have my meals cooked by your vulture-headed all-purpose Egyptian goddess. Good afternoon.'

The door slammed. Next door, the dean jumped. 'Dear me, dear me, Bonaccord's started it now,' he muttered.

The psychiatrist gave a sigh. 'I'm afraid that was a most distressing scene for you, Miss MacNish.'

'I'm perfectly used to Sir Lancelot, Doctor. Sometimes he gets quite beside himself, over absolutely nothing at all.'

'Really? You mean he loses control?'

'Oh, yes. Becomes violent, too.'

'Indeed? That's interesting. Very interesting. Any other peculiarities?'

'Crawling with them, Doctor. Like an old sheep with ticks.'

'Perhaps I should have put him on tranquillizers,' said Dr Bonaccord thoughtfully. 'It might have been safer for the street.'

'*You* don't object to my pets, do you, Doctor?'

'Not at all. I think a fondness for cats is very civilized – dogs after all are rather vulgar. Did you know that killing a cat in ancient Egypt was punishable by death? And to the Romans, of course, the cat was the symbol of liberty.'

'Who'd have thought it, Doctor?'

'I hope you're settling in comfortably? You'll find our top floor flat much like the one you've just left down the road.'

'I'm sorry to give Mrs Tennant the inconvenience of moving out, Doctor.'

'I'm sure she doesn't really mind in the least. She's overjoyed at having someone as reliable as yourself to take the household duties off her hands. And her new bedroom is really quite pleasant.'

Dr Bonaccord went upstairs to his own bedroom, which was plain white picked out in gold. On the double bed sat Gisela, legs drawn up on the white candlewick, gold-flecked bedspread, idly turning over the shiny pages of a pornographic magazine.

'Where'd you get this, Cedric?'

'The Swedish one, is it? People send them to me from time to time for a psychiatric opinion. Schoolmasters, vicars, those sort of persons. They're usually pretty thumbed through.'

'What do you think of *that*?'

'Oh, it looks rather fun.'

'But do you think they could actually be enjoying it?'

'I don't suppose people actually enjoy scaling mountains. But it makes an exciting change from the ordinary, which is better.'

'It's a wonder she doesn't break a leg.'

Shutting the bedroom door, he sat down beside her. He turned the page. 'Have you ever done it like that, Gissie?'

She gave a little shriek. 'Of course not? Have you?'

'I doubt whether many people have. They haven't the space in a modern house, and they'd be afraid the neighbours might hear. All that these publications really illustrate are the readers' fantasies.' He flicked over more pages. *'L'amour...n'est que l'échange de deux fantaisies et le contact de deux épidermes.* Chamfort was right about the whole business. Thank God I am above all the stupid self-delusions, self-persecutions and self-denials which others so delightedly wallow in. By the way, that stupid old buffer Sir Lancelot was asking after your husband.'

'Oh?'

'He claimed to have met him last winter in Sydney.'

'That would be clever.'

'Yes, it would.'

'What did you say?'

'I made some remark putting him on another trail.'

She hesitated. 'Do you suppose he's suspicious?'

'Why should he be, particularly? He honestly imagined he'd met the fellow. He was mistaken, but he was rationalizing his lapse of memory.'

'One day, you know, someone's going to stumble on to the truth about my husband.'

'But why?'

'People are naturally curious.'

'They're also naturally lazy. They never put themselves out to discover things of little immediate importance to themselves.'

'I only hope you're right, Cedric.'

'I generally am in my assessment of human nature. Because I always expect it to operate at its basest.'

She shut the magazine and slipped it in a bedside drawer. 'But what do you imagine they think at the hospital of our being together here? Particularly now I'm not even keeping up the pretence of living in the flat.'

'They'll think what they've always thought. After all, we're both highly attractive. A lot of people would like to find themselves in bed with either of us. Or with both of us, perhaps.'

'Who would? Sir Lancelot?'

They laughed. 'How do you like that next-door bedroom, Gissie?'

'Everything pink, rounded, and soft... I've always thought it utterly womblike.'

'What do you think of this one?'

'Virginal.'

'The white...a pleasant association of ideas.' He ran his hand softly up her arm. 'What about this new Scots oddbody we've acquired?'

'She'll do the cooking, which I loathed and was anyway hopeless at.'

'Do you suppose she'll assume we sleep together?'

'She does already, from what I know of our neighbours.'

'Yes, they're a vinegary lot of gossips. But all neighbours hate each other, according to Freud. I know Jesus was inclined to an opposite view, but I'm more ready to accept a qualified opinion.' He paused. 'Then if she thinks we sleep together...why don't we?'

She stared at him reproachfully. 'Oh, Cedric...'

'Why do you sound so hurt?'

'I couldn't do that. No, I couldn't.'

'You know I've wanted you to, don't you? Often. However hard I've tried to keep it to myself.'

She nodded, dropping her eyes. 'Of course I've noticed how you've looked at me sometimes, at night.'

'My eyes filled with good healthy lust? Well, Gissie, what's wrong with that? A sound, well-established psychological reaction at finding yourself alone with a beautiful, charming and incredibly sexy female.'

'Please don't go on, Cedric. Talk of anything else about us, but not *that* in particular.'

He put his hands on her shoulders, slowly drawing her to him. 'You do know exactly how I feel, don't you? I say "exactly" advisedly. Because I know you feel the same, the precise same, towards me. That's right, isn't it?'

She put her head back, her eyes closed.

'That's right, isn't it?' he repeated.

She nodded almost imperceptibly. He held her tightly. They kissed, with a passion untapped in their casual embraces round the house.

'But I won't rape you.' He stood up abruptly. 'Nor even seduce you, which would be less exciting but quieter. I shan't even mention the idea again – unless you do.' She shook her head vigorously. 'You're quite a little prude at heart, aren't you?'

'Do you have to torment me about it as well?'

'I'm sorry. Perhaps I was a little surprised at you, after all this time. We shall go on our happy little ways, exactly as before. I can control myself. I am balanced. I see my own mind with a professional eye. I sometimes think that psychiatry really cures very few patients, but is incredibly good treatment for the psychiatrists.'

She looked at him imploringly. 'You're not cross with me, are you?'

'Not a bit. I must now go and put a final note on old Sir Lancelot's file while I remember. I seem to have cured him – I hope not too successfully. He might become hooked on cats, and go round the district stealing them. That could cause a great deal of embarrassment at the hospital.' Dr Bonaccord paused at the bedroom door. 'That dream of his – banging nails into ebony. I mean... phew!'

16

'Odd,' mused the dean. 'Distinctly odd.' He was staring through the front downstairs window of No 2, towards seven-thirty that evening. The door was open leading to the small inner dining-room, where he could hear his wife putting final touches to the dinner-table.

'What's odd?' she called.

'Another one. Just gone past the end of the street. Odd.'

'Another what, dear?'

'Pregnant woman. Do you know, until this morning I never seemed to set eyes on an expectant mother from one year's end to the other. Now they're suddenly all over the place. I swear I bumped into half a dozen when I stepped out to buy some books this afternoon. As for St Swithin's, the place seems one enormous antenatal clinic. I remember, I noticed exactly the same when you were having George and Muriel. Perhaps I ought to have a word with Bonaccord about it.'

'I suppose it's like when you've been caught for speeding. You see policemen staring at you everywhere.'

'Quite. When my old auntie died last winter, every street in London seemed a traffic-jam of funerals.'

The dean's eyes widened a little behind his large glasses. A faint, gratified smile played on his lips. Leaving a taxi on the corner was Frankie Humble.

He watched unseen as the MP trotted past his window, mounted the steps of No 3 and rang the bell. He had telephoned her the previous evening, throwing himself on her mercy. The appointment at Hampton Wick, he pleaded, would be less a tragedy than a black farce for a man of

95

his own sensitivity, humanity, conscientiousness, kindness, good-humour, malleability, fairness, high-mindedness, culture, responsibility and tendency to rheumatism when chilled. He would break even sooner than the others – much sooner than the tough Australian. Not only would Hampton Wick suffer but – though, of course, this would be a minor consideration entirely – his own career would be in ruins at St Swithin's.

What Frankie needed was a strong man, he urged. An academic Cromwell – or possibly an academic Hitler. Someone tough of mind, body and voice. Someone in the lifelong habit of dominating, of getting his own way, of squashing opposition so flat the breath remained out of it for weeks. Someone not too fancy with his manners or his language, who could sink with ease to the puerile level of students' humour. In short, Sir Lancelot Spratt.

Frankie had demurred. The official announcement was already prepared for release after the weekend. But the dean sounded so piteous she agreed at least to see Sir Lancelot, and put the idea to him. 'I'll try to persuade him,' she promised. 'But if I don't, I'll expect you to keep your word. I'm sure you wouldn't like it to get round London that you ratted, would you?' The dean agreed readily. When Frankie persuaded anyone to perform anything she really wanted, it was as good as done.

The dean watched her disappear inside. 'Well, there's Miss MacNish about the place to keep an eye on the pair of them,' he murmured to himself, still smiling. 'They need a chaperone, if you ask me. I wouldn't put anything entirely past Frankie, especially with her husband away…and I certainly wouldn't put it past Sir Lancelot, if she gets him in the right mood.' His face took on a thoughtful look. He pulled his right earlobe. 'I wonder, when Frankie was his house-surgeon, if Sir Lancelot ever *did*…' He paused. 'And I wonder if he wonders if I ever did…'

'Aren't you going to open the wine, Lionel?' called his wife from the next room. 'The young man will be here any minute.'

'What are we having before the roast beef?'

'Asparagus and plovers' eggs.'

The dean jumped. 'Have you thought of the expense? We're

entertaining our future son-in-law, not some wealthy hospital benefactor.'

'I just fancied them. After all, we must make some sort of show. You wouldn't like him to think we couldn't afford a treat now and then, would you?'

The dean went through the hall to the kitchen and opened a bottle of supermarket beaujolais. For a wild moment he considered uncorking the champagne, which had been replaced in the refrigerator the evening before. But he decided it would be more economical to keep it for the wedding, or possibly the birth of the baby.

He went with the bottle to the dining-room, where his wife was arranging a bowl of sweet-peas in the middle of the table. 'I just saw Frankie go past,' the dean told her. 'She didn't lose any time making a date with Lancelot.'

'Oh? What was she wearing?'

'A sort of black thing with holes in it. Rather fetching, actually.'

'You'd think Frankie Humble fetching if she were dressed in an old potato-sack, wouldn't you?'

The dean looked startled. 'I hadn't really visualized the situation.'

'Though of course you'd prefer her in nothing at all.'

'Josephine! What a thing to say to your husband. The dean of St Swithin's, too.'

'Well, it's perfectly true. You drool even when you speak to her over the telephone.'

'Of course I don't.' He sounded outraged. 'One must be reasonably polite.'

'You go out drinking with her –'

'I can hardly refuse to be sociable –'

'You let her do what she likes with you –'

'As a Member of Parliament her wishes must to some extent be respected –'

'Nonsense, Lionel. It was exactly the same when she was your house-physician. You were the scandal of the hospital.'

'I have a duty to encourage the young in my own profession –'

'You've got a medical Lolita syndrome, that's your trouble. What do you care about me? Nothing! You don't even look at me these days. Not even when I'm in the bath.'

The dean's voice trembled nervously. 'My dear, I assure you I entertain exactly the same feelings for you as on our wedding-night.'

'When you had a horrible cold and I had to tuck you up with aspirin and hot lemon.'

'Well, the next night,' the dean conceded. 'Or whenever it was I felt strong enough.'

'Now you never even take me out to dinner.'

'But Josephine, you had a wonderful time at the students' May ball.'

'A whole month ago. And it was Sir Lancelot's party, anyway.'

'We'll go out on Monday and dance all night, if you like.' He was mystified at the unexpected outburst. 'I never knew you were suffering from such feelings, not for one minute. And it's so unlike you, just to break down like this. I've always looked on you as a tower of strength. A very well-constructed and decorative tower, of course.'

'Oh, Lionel!' She burst into tears, throwing herself at him.

'There, there!' The dean patted her vigorously. 'Come, come! Now, now! You're not quite yourself today, my dear, that's all. It's the strain we're all going through, isn't it?'

She blew her nose. 'I expect that's it. It's such an awful worry about Muriel. And so dreadfully sudden.'

'We shall just have to make the best of it, that's all.' He smiled. 'Though perhaps you're right, Josephine. I'm not sufficiently attentive to you. Not as you so richly and rightly deserve. But it's so difficult, with so many things on my mind… Now I promise I'll be a little more…er, vigorous. Let's say, next Saturday. Not of course that the weekend should make any difference, but one gets so used to dividing one's work from one's pleasure. I mean, at the weekend one mows the lawn and so on… Yes, definitely Saturday night. You will remind me, won't you? I do get so dreadfully tired these days.'

'Lionel, you're very sweet. I'm sorry that I seemed to lose control of myself all of a sudden.' She dabbed her eyes with the edge of a table-napkin. 'Edgar will be here any minute. I must look reasonably pleased with life.'

The door bell rang. The dean heard Muriel hurrying down from her flat, where she had been sulking most of the afternoon. There was a crash from the house next door. The dean jumped. 'Great heavens! What on earth is Lancelot doing to Frankie? Throwing her downstairs?'

17

'Clumsy!' said Frankie with a smile.

Sir Lancelot looked ruefully at the trayful of smashed crockery at his feet. 'Really, Frankie, it's hopeless trying to turn myself into a butler at this stage of my life. And, I would add, at this stage of the evening.'

Frankie picked Miss MacNish's flowered apron from a hook in the kitchen and tied it round her in a businesslike way. 'I said I'd cook our dinner, and cook it I shall. I'm sure you've got lots more plates and things somewhere? I expect you can glue some of that lot together later. Though it would probably be less trouble to sweep it up and put it in the dustbin.'

'Why don't we go to a restaurant, as I suggested? Or if you like, there's a place round the corner where the students take away packets of fish and chips.'

'Just pour me another of those huge vodkas, my darling, and leave the rest to me.'

'You know this is genuine vodka, don't you? It was given me by a patient from the Russian Embassy.'

'Never drink anything else.'

'I imagine they use it for thawing out the tundra.'

'Has that tergiversating cook of yours left any food in the house?'

'I believe there's some fillets of steak.'

'You've cream and mushrooms and onions? I'll do you a perfect *boeuf strogonoff*. It'll go with the vodka.'

When Sir Lancelot reappeared with two ice-clinking tumblers, Frankie was already busy with the frying-pan. As she took the glass with a smile, he noticed that characteristic little twitch of her nose. It always sent delightful shivers up and down his vertebrae.

'A nice little perch you've come to roost on here, Lancelot.'

'I should have invited you here long ago, my dear. But I imagined you too busy. You always seem to be in the news.'

'Oh, the news.' She twitched her nose again. The ice jangled in Sir Lancelot's glass. 'There's too much of it. "The news expands to fill the media", that's my motto. People gawp at it from the moment they open their eyes until they switch off the telly and go to bed. The world would be a far more tranquil place if we returned to broadsheets on the walls of public houses.'

'I sometimes wish that I had tried my hand at politics.'

'Do you?' She looked surprised. 'You're far too good a doctor.'

'Well, perhaps too experienced a one.'

The strips of steak were sizzling gently in butter. 'Doctors see problems clearly and unemotionally, Lancelot. In politics, we see them only according to our point of view. It's like a case of pneumonia being diagnosed by a neuro-surgeon as a slipped disc and a dermatologist as shingles. No wonder the world lurches so paralytically along the road to the millennium.'

'It must be gratifying to contribute something to the running of the country, beyond one's taxes.'

'Taxes! More power for the state. And the modern state is a jealous god.' She added the mushrooms. 'Middle-class individualists like you are doomed, I'm afraid. Even now, most of the specimens of your species are safely fossilized, squashed flat in the deeper economic strata.'

'I'm not sure if I should be only offended by that, or depressed.'

'Depressed.' In went the cream. 'Liberty is outdated. Or rather, the state provides it like the drains – as a necessity to keep the population reasonably healthy, but channelled and under continual and painstaking supervision by experts who know best. Do get me another vodka.'

As he came back with more drinks, she was busy with a serving-dish. 'Delighted as I am to see you Frankie, you haven't yet even hinted at the reason for inviting yourself.'

'I shall keep that as a surprise till you've had your dinner. I don't want anything to distract your mind from my cooking.'

'I assure you that nothing on earth could distract it from you yourself.'

'What a sweet man you are.' A high-pitched cackling noise came from next door. 'What on earth's that?'

'The dean must be giving a party,' said Sir Lançelot glumly. 'He will have told his one funny story. He always laughs at it heartily himself.'

The dean's dinner-party was not much of a success. Edgar Sharpewhistle sat eating steadily and silently, drinking all the beaujolais. Muriel gave the impression of imagining she was dining alone. The dean told his story. Only Josephine showed any animation.

'I'm really terribly thrilled about the baby. In fact, it's making me quite broody myself. Of course, I'll do all I can to help you, my dear. And naturally, your father will pay for the baby-clothes and the pram and the cot and all the things like that. Won't you, Lionel?'

'Within –'

'He'll be delighted to. Have you thought where you're going to have it?'

Muriel looked even gloomier. 'St Swithin's, I suppose.'

'Good God, no,' muttered the dean. 'Why not go somewhere deep into the country? I mean, where it's much quieter. You get no sleep at all in a London hospital these days.'

'Of course you'll have it in St Swithin's. I can't go traipsing up and down to the country with my bad back. But we've the wedding to think of first. Are you sure you can fix it with the local registry office so soon? We'll have to ask a few close friends, of course. And there's no reason why we shouldn't have a rather magnificent reception afterwards, which of course your father will pay for.'

'Within –'

'It's your *privilege*, Lionel. Then you've got to find somewhere to live. All the linen and the household goods will of course be provided by your father –'

'Within –'

'So that's one less of your many worries. And naturally he'll give you something for the bank, to start you off the right way.'

'Within –'

'Lionel, I do wish you wouldn't keep interrupting when I'm trying to give the happy couple some good advice.'

'I suppose you really do want to go ahead with this elaborate programme?' suggested the dean hopefully.

'You mean, not to get married?' Edgar Sharpewhistle broke his silence. 'Ah, I see. Not to give our child a name? Or perhaps just to get rid of it?' He glared aggressively, fortified by the beaujolais. No one said anything. 'It's going to be a genius, too. Can't help it, can it? Not with Muriel and self as parents. We've got the best genes in the business, you might say. It might be another Beethoven. Another Newton. Another Churchill. I'm ashamed at you, dad. May I call you dad? I'm ashamed of you for suggesting such a despicable act. The dean of my own hospital, too.'

'Let's have some brandy,' said the dean quickly.

They sat in the front room. Sharpewhistle managed to keep the brandy bottle near his elbow, helping himself. Muriel stared gloomily ahead in silence. Josephine concentrated on her embroidery. The dean had the idea of locking the brandy away in the kitchen cupboard, but felt for once the stronger impulse of keeping it handy for himself.

'Do you know, dad, what my IQ is?' Sharpewhistle asked expansively. 'Over a hundred and fifty. I'm off the chart. Over the top. What's yours?'

'I don't know.'

'You must do.'

'I haven't got one,' the dean told him gloomily. 'When I was at school they hadn't been invented.' He helped himself to another drink. He suddenly wondered what Sir Lancelot and Frankie were up to. It had been noticeably silent next door for some time.

Sir Lancelot was sitting in his armchair, drinking port. Frankie was on his knee, a glass of benedictine in one hand, stroking his neck with the other. 'It would be a great honour, Lancelot,' she murmured.

He looked solemn. 'Indeed, a vice-chancellorship would certainly be a fitting crown to my career.'

'Very fitting. Remember, five years ago when the university was founded, you wanted so much to be its very first vice-chancellor?'

'True…'

'And Hampton Wick wouldn't take you far from St Swithin's. You wouldn't miss your old haunts.'

'Does anyone else know about this offer?'

'Not a soul. As soon as the vacancy came before the committee, I told myself, "Only Lancelot Spratt has the stature to fill such an important – and indeed, testing – position in the academic world." '

'You really thought that?'

'I thought more than that. I thought, "if Lancelot cannot come to our rescue, then Hampton Wick must close its doors. The careers of thousands of young people will be ruined".'

'That's very touching.'

'You think so?'

'Though doubtless they could find alternative work as demolition experts, assault troops and so on.'

'Will you take the job?'

He said nothing.

'*Please* Lancelot, dear. For me.'

He still said nothing. Then she happened to twitch her nose.

He gave a sigh. 'I accept.'

'Dear Lancelot!' She kissed him lightly on the beard. 'An official announcement will be made on Monday. In fact, I was so sure you'd gallantly come to my rescue, that I've drafted it already.' She got up, draining her benedictine. 'Now I must fly.'

'Must you?' He looked deeply disappointed. 'But surely, Frankie, you can tarry a little longer? After all these years… I mean, we're both worldly and sophisticated,' he added hopefully. 'And we are, I think, both enthusiastic hedonists – '

'Good heavens no, Lancelot. Not tonight. I've got a three-line whip.'

He stood up. 'I shall get very lonely, you know, all by myself. Even Miss MacNish was someone to talk to. It's rather pathetic, I suppose.'

'Poor Lancelot!' She was adjusting her make-up.

'It's not easy to seek out another woman in my busy life.'

'Why don't you go to an agency?'

'I know nothing of such things.'

'It's hardly an exercise demanding brains or study. That's the object of them. Try Hotblack's in Burlington Street.'

'Hotblack's? Is it reliable?'

'Some of my friends who've used it say so.'

'Never heard of them,' he grumbled.

'You don't get around enough, dear.' She stroked his beard with a smile. 'Give them a try. After all, you don't *have* to accept whoever they recommend.'

Sir Lancelot opened the front door. Offering his arm with a flourish, he escorted her to the corner of Lazar Row for a taxi.

He turned towards his house pensively. It was a clear warm night, just becoming dark. He saw a shaft of light as the dean's front door opened. A small figure hurried past, calling to him, 'Good night, sir.' Sir Lancelot frowned. As he came abreast of No 2, the dean was standing in the doorway. 'Who was that?'

'Why, it's Lancelot, my dear fellow. Dear old Lancelot. That was Sharpewhistle.'

'The bum-faced student?'

'Exactly.'

'What's *he* doing in your house, for God's sake.'

'He's going to marry my daughter.'

'Good God.'

The dean came down to the pavement, holding on to the area railings. 'Edgar and Muriel.'

'The two contenders for the gold medal, eh?' mused Sir Lancelot. 'That should be a marriage pregnant with possibilities.'

'Har! How did you know?'

'Know what?'

'She's preggers.'

'Is she?'

'You just said so.'

'I didn't.'

'Don't try getting out of it now.' The dean wagged a finger violently. 'Insult me as much as you like, but don't besmirch my daughter. Anyway, all girls are pregnant these days. When they get married, that is.'

'So Sharpewhistle put her in the family way? Well, well. I wouldn't have thought he had it in him. A nice girl like Muriel, too.'

'It was after your blasted party,' said the dean with sudden anger. 'All your sexy champagne.'

'What did you expect me to do? Serve the pill as a canapé?'

'Anyway, there it is. I'm lumbered with Sharpewhistle for life. The baby will probably look half like me and half like him. God!'

They looked up towards the brightening stars as a light flashed on overhead. The psychiatrist was going to bed.. 'Odd sod, Bonaccord,' observed the dean.

'He has managed to organize his life very comfortably.'

'You mean the secretary?'

'Well…partly.'

'I expect he's having a slice of her now.'

Sir Lancelot frowned. 'How much have you been drinking tonight?'

'A lot. To put up with Sharpewhistle. I shall have to continue drinking as long as I have to look at him. So apart from anything else, the bloody man has turned me into a chronic alcoholic.'

Sir Lancelot's thoughts were elsewhere. 'There's something very peculiar about Mrs Tennant. Or rather about her husband. She's very evasive about the fellow.'

'Probably in jail.'

'Maybe. And where did she come from, anyway? She told me once she'd been secretary to the professor of psychiatry at High Cross. I ran into the old fruitcake himself last month, and he'd never heard of her.'

'Could be she wasn't married then. Girls change their names. Like Lychfield to Sharpewhistle. What a bloody name! It sounds like a direction to engine drivers.'

'At least they've got Miss MacNish to look after them now,' continued Sir Lancelot sourly. 'It's absolutely unfair, Bonaccord living in sin with first-class cuisine and comforts.'

The dean stared at him. 'When did that happen?'

'I asked for her resignation this afternoon.'

'So you've been alone in there half the night with Frankie?'

'What of it?'

'But it's quite…quite… Her husband away in South America, too.'

'How did you know that?' asked Sir Lancelot narrowly.

'It's in all the papers,' the dean replied hastily. 'Didn't you notice? I say…Lancelot…'

'Yes?'

'Er…did you?'

'No.'

'I mean, ever?'

'No.'

There was a pause.

'Lionel?'

'Yes?'

'Did *you*?'

'Never. Wouldn't let me.'

'Nor me.'

'Honest?'

'Honest.'

'Often wondered, you know.'

'So did I about you.' They stood looking at each other, the dean still clasping the railings. 'Can I tell you a secret, Lionel?'

'Of course. Professional discretion, and all that thing.'

'I shall be leaving Lazar Row.'

'No?'

'In October.'

'No!'

'I'm taking another job.'

'Well! This is a surprise.'

Sir Lancelot threw out his chest. 'I have been offered the vice-chancellorship of the university of Hampton Wick.'

'Really? Good heavens! You *have* definitely accepted it?' the dean asked anxiously.

'Aren't you going to congratulate me?'

'With all my heart. With all my heart.'

'It was Frankie, of course. She seems to have the appointment at her disposal.'

'Never knew that.'

'She's very interested in education, of course.'

'Go on? Never knew that, either.'

'You think I was right to take the job?'

'Would never have had a moment's hesitation myself.'

'It's not going to be a cushy one. Quite the opposite.'

'Nothing to a man of your qualities, Lancelot.'

'Possibly I have something of a flair for handling the young. I wanted to be their first vice-chancellor, you know, five years ago.'

'So Frankie told me.'

'Oh? When were *you* discussing it, pray?'

'Chit-chat, you know, at some party or other.'

'An official announcement will be made on Monday.'

'And no one, my dear Lancelot, will read it with deeper emotion than myself.'

'That's very handsome of you.' He hesitated. 'You're a very decent chap, you know, Lionel.'

'And so are you, Lancelot. So are you. In fact, I think I would say about you – "His brusque exterior, though known by many generations of students at St Swithin's to conceal a heart of gold, was perceived only by his fortunate intimates to cover, as the bark of a sturdy tree, a sap indistinguishable from the milk of human kindness".'

'And I think I would say about you – "The image of cold, classical intellect he presented to the world was appreciated only by those blessed with his close friendship as a mere mask to hide a bubbling conviviality".'

'That's very nice of you, Lancelot.'

'It's nice of you, too, Lionel. Though you do make me sound like a Malaysian rubber-tree. Well, good night.'

'Good night, old man. I would also say that your unfailing optimism and sound commonsense were invaluable to your friends in their own adversities.'

'And I would say, "Never was there a kinder, more generous and more thoughtful father and husband".'

'Good night.'

'Good night.'

'I do wish those two bloody old fools would turn off,' muttered Dr Bonaccord into his pillow.

18

Shortly after nine o'clock the following morning a small green van swung round the corner from the main road and jerked to a stop outside the front door of No 3 Lazar Row. On its side was painted in yellow *Flowers For All Occasions*. Indeed, the small florist's opposite the hospital gates could supply almost instantly bunches suitable for long or short illnesses, for accidents or for childbirth, and always carried a varied stock of wreaths.

The driver was a fair girl in a pink smock, who emerged with a large bouquet of orange gladioli. She rang the bell. Sir Lancelot appeared, in his black coat and striped trousers.

'Very good of you to deliver so quickly after my phone call,' he thanked her.

'Not at all, Sir Lancelot. We'd do anything for you. After all, in a way we share the same customers, don't we?'

'H'm,' said Sir Lancelot.

As the van drove off he started along the short cul-de-sac. At that moment the door of No 2. was flung open and the dean strode out, looking bad-tempered.

'Morning, dean,' said Sir Lancelot amiably. 'You were pissed last night.'

'Not at all. I had been eating plovers' eggs, which have a peculiar effect on me. Anyway, they were bad. They've certainly upset Josephine this morning. Where are you going with those flowers? Off to see Frankie Humble, I suppose?'

'My dear dean, every doctor should have a healthily suspicious mind. But this time your diagnosis is wrong. As I woke this morning I happened to remember it was Miss MacNish's birthday. It would seem petty and churlish of me to shun marking it as usual.'

'How are you managing to look after yourself?'

'I am not. I never realized that boiling an egg was an operation of such intricacy. But I hope the situation will shortly resolve itself.'

'Perhaps the hospital can find you someone living locally?'

'I don't want to train two separate people to my ways. I shall be leaving here in October, remember. But not a word about Hampton Wick to anybody, until Monday.'

'Oh, not a word. Nobody knows about me, either.'

'I beg your pardon?'

'I mean... I'm a man of mystery, aren't I?'

The dean gave a weak smile, and quickened his pace towards the hospital. Sir Lancelot rang the bell of No 1. Almost immediately the door was opened by Dr Bonaccord himself.

'For me?' he asked humorously.

'It is my former cook's birthday. Perhaps I can present them myself?'

'Of course. You'll find her through the back somewhere. By the way, those trout were delicious. I hope they're still biting next time you go fishing.'

'They do not bite. They suck.'

'Really? Well, good luck at it. That's all a fisherman needs, isn't it? Now I'm afraid I must be off on my bicycle to St Swithin's.'

Miss MacNish was in the kitchen, blue overall sleeves turned up to the elbows, vigorously polishing a silver serving-dish. She looked startled as Sir Lancelot entered, but quickly changed her expression to one of polite, impersonal enquiry. 'Were you looking for the doctor, sir? I think he's just left.'

'Many happy returns of the day.'

'Thank you, sir. I'll put them in water.'

'Gladioli – your favourite flowers. You see, I hadn't forgotten.'

'Several of my former employers still send me birthday cards, sir.'

'Miss MacNish, you were possibly a little overwrought yesterday afternoon. I am prepared to disregard everything.'

'Thank you, sir.'

Sir Lancelot looked round anxiously. There was no sign of vermin. 'How are the cats?'

'They have a good home, sir.'

'Perhaps I myself behaved over-impulsively. I assure you I really think them the most delightful cats.'

'Dr Bonaccord does not pick them up by their tails, sir.'

'I really meant it no harm whatever. It was a game – almost a joke. I'm sure they are lovely companions to you, and of great value in exterminating the mice. It is simply that I have a thing about cats.'

'So it would seem, sir.'

'Miss MacNish, you obliged me to expose that I have some sort of psychological allergy to cats. But luckily I have with Dr Bonaccord's help been able to overcome it. Nothing would so complete my comfort in the evening, as I sit with my whisky and a book, than my slippered feet on a large, well-fed purring cat.'

She went on with the silver dish.

'Miss MacNish, come back to me.'

'No, sir.'

'But surely! Isn't all forgiven?'

'*I* forgive you, sir. I know that some of us have difficulty in controlling our bestial instincts. But little Chelsea hasn't forgiven you. I can tell that, from the look in its eyes.'

'I am quite prepared to exist in a state of odium *vis-à-vis* your cats.'

'No, sir. It won't do, sir. I am perfectly well suited, thank you, sir.'

He became impatient. 'Really, Miss MacNish! You can't go on working in this...this disorderly house.' She raised her eyebrows. 'How can a lady of your propriety, of your purity, of your Presbyterianism, allow herself to remain in an establishment which reeks of sin like St Swithin's reeks of antiseptic?'

'I don't think I understand what you mean, sir.'

'You don't suppose Dr Bonaccord has Mrs Tennant only to stick his insurance stamps on, do you?'

'That is a most unpleasant inference, sir.'

'It isn't an inference. Everyone in St Swithin's knows it for a fact. I'm surprised at someone like you, Miss MacNish, shutting your eyes to it.'

'I do not shut my eyes to anything. On the contrary, Sir Lancelot, I keep them wide open. And I have seen nothing whatever in this house to justify your slur.'

'But damn it, you've only been here one night.'

'I can tell these things, Sir Lancelot. I believe Dr Bonaccord and the young lady are chaste, strictly speaking. One can find out a lot about people very quickly when you serve them and look after them. Until I come across definite evidence to the contrary, I am more than ready to be charitable and give them the benefit of the doubt.'

'Miss MacNish, you're a simpleton.'

'Sir Lancelot, you have a dirty mind.'

'This is getting quite out of hand. You must return to the nest immediately.'

'I will not.'

'But don't you realize how I'm floundering, woman? I haven't the first idea how to set about making my own bed.'

'You should have thought about that before you started pulling up cats by their tails.'

'Are you or are you not coming with me?'

'No. Would you like the flowers back, sir?'

He turned away with a mixture of despair, frustration, the pains of ingratitude, and offended pride. 'You said you discovered a lot about people when you kept house for them. I assume that applies also to me?'

'You? Oh, yes, Sir Lancelot. It would take a book.'

She went on polishing more vigorously than ever. He grunted and pushed open the kitchen door. Immediately outside was Gisela Tennant. 'It is Miss MacNish's birthday,' he told her quickly.

The secretary eyed him coldly. He supposed she must have overheard most of the conversation, and quite deliberately. 'I'm glad you could find time to pay a call on her, Sir Lancelot.'

'Though I had nothing of particular importance to tell her. Nothing at all.'

'I'm sure not.'

Sir Lancelot shifted awkwardly from one foot to the other. 'I met the professor of psychiatry from High Cross the other day. I believe you worked as his secretary before you married?'

'I should prefer not to discuss my marriage. It is a most painful subject.'

'I'm extremely sorry...'

'Anyway, my husband is not in Australia, but the Australian territories of New Guinea. I don't expect you penetrated as far as there?' Her eyes widened an instant as she noticed Sir Lancelot begin to tremble. His glance searched round wildly. Chelsea, the fat black one, was slowly coming downstairs. With a faint smile, Gisela watched him clench his fists to take control of himself. The cat paused at the foot of the stairs. It looked hard at Sir Lancelot, as if knowing the inner convulsions it was causing. Then it pushed the part-open door to the kitchen and its benefactress. 'You would seem to be improving, Sir Lancelot,' Gisela said, with muted but distinct derision.

'I freely admit that Dr Bonaccord did me considerable good.'

'I'm sure he will appreciate the compliment as much as I do. We're both aware that you entertain a somewhat low opinion of psychiatrists.'

'That's not at all fair,' he said crossly.

'No? Well, perhaps all the remarks attributed to you on the subject have been invented maliciously. It is quite remarkable what one can learn about oneself from the chance overhearing of scraps of conversation. Things that are not only surprising, but absolutely flabbergasting in their inaccuracy. I should like you to know, Sir Lancelot, that Dr Bonaccord is a widely-respected and very influential man.'

'I have nothing against his professional abilities whatever.'

'So much so, Sir Lancelot, that he was offered the vice-chancellorship of a university only last week.'

Sir Lancelot started. 'Bonaccord? What an amazing coincidence.'

'He was approached by a Member of Parliament, and you might be interested to know that he so nearly accepted that an official announcement was to be made to the effect on Monday next. But in the end Dr Bonaccord felt he could do more with his life by continuing to treat the mentally sick at St Swithin's.'

'Was it – Hampton Wick?'

'That's curious. You are quite right, and it was supposed to be a dead secret. What's the matter, Sir Lancelot? Another cat?'

'If you'll forgive me… I must be getting along… already late for St Swithin's…'

Gisela opened the front door. 'It's always a pleasure to see you, Sir Lancelot. But should you wish again to enjoy a chat with Miss MacNish at her work, perhaps you would kindly inform me first? After all, as Dr Bonaccord's secretary the running of the house and management of staff is entirely my responsibility. If you wish to amuse yourself by conversing with her in her spare time, of course that is entirely up to her. Good morning.'

She shut the door. She tightened her lips. She strode into the kitchen.

'What are those flowers doing? I didn't give you permission to order any flowers.'

'Sir Lancelot brought them, Mrs Tennant. For me.'

'Oh. Why are you polishing that dish?'

'You wouldn't like it to be tarnished, would you?'

'I don't like it in any shape or form. It's far too old-fashioned.'

'Sir Lancelot always said that good food deserved to be presented on silver.'

'And I saw you took Dr Bonaccord's breakfast coffee-cup from his study this morning. You are not to go in there without my permission, if you please.'

'I'm sure Sir Lancelot wouldn't have cared to find dirty crockery lying among his papers.'

'That's exactly the point. A psychiatrist's papers are extremely confidential. By the way, my personal papers are in the desk on the landing. It is always locked.'

Miss MacNish went on polishing. 'I'm not the prying kind, Mrs Tennant, thank you very much.'

'I'm sure you're not, but it's best that we get our respective attitudes clear from the start.'

'Sir Lancelot always trusted me.'

'I'm sure that we can, too – and not to discuss either of us behind our backs. Dr Bonaccord will be in for dinner tonight. At eight o'clock, please.'

'Sir Lancelot always dined at seven.'

'Miss MacNish, since you arrived here less than twenty-four hours ago, you have informed me of Sir Lancelot's likes and dislikes every twenty minutes, regularly. We are delighted you have decided to work for us, and we both highly appreciate you, but we are not in the slightest interested in any of Sir Lancelot's habits.'

'I'm just trying to provide the doctor with service in the way I am accustomed.'

'I think I know Dr Bonaccord's likes and dislikes well enough. It is only necessary for you to listen to me on the subject.'

'I am not accustomed, Mrs Tennant, to listen to my gentlemen's secretaries on any subject.' She put the dish in a cupboard with a clang.

Gisela stared at her, shrugged her shoulders, and left. She went back to the front room, where her portable typewriter was ready on the table beside a pile of letters. She hitched up her skirt and sat down. 'I wonder,' she asked herself, 'if that will do the trick? I was really most wonderfully rude. Well, she flounced in upon us. So she may as easily flounce out again.'

She put a sheet of paper in the machine and started to work. She could never bear the intrusion of even a shadow between herself and Cedric Bonaccord.

19

'Hotblack's,' said Sir Lancelot.

He climbed into the back of the taxi. It was twenty minutes later. He should have been starting an outpatients' clinic at St Swithin's, but he had telephoned his registrar to take it instead. It was a ridiculous waste of time, he thought, going down to an employment agency in the West End. But it was an even more ludicrous waste making his own bed and cleaning the floors. I'm a surgeon, he told himself, not a scrubwoman.

The cab stopped at a plain doorway in a dignified stone building at the back of the Burlington House, not far from the bespoke tailors who provided Sir Lancelot with his formal suits and – unflinchingly – his hairy ginger tweeds. A metal plate beside the door said simply, *Hotblack's*. 'Looks respectable,' he muttered, and strode in.

Through an inner glass door was a small, plain office furnished in the inhibited Regency-gentility style of a Harley Street waiting-room. Behind a table with a pair of telephones and a leather-bound diary a young dark-haired girl in a stylish dress eyed him with a mixture of disdain and frank hostility. 'Have you got an appointment?'

'Of course not. Did I need one?'

'It's customary to telephone first.'

Sir Lancelot stifled his irritation. These days, any tuppenny business seemed to assume toward the public the airs rightful to consultant surgeons. 'I'm sorry. I imagined that would simply complicate matters. I want you to supply me with a woman as soon as possible.'

'What!'

Sir Lancelot stared at her. 'I should imagine you have adequate numbers on your books?'

'Well…yes. But it isn't usually fixed up instantly, you know.'

'I don't want to take her away with me here and now, of course. Not if that would be inconvenient. But I should certainly like her before tonight.'

The girl slowly fanned herself with a sheet of typing paper. 'You're a cool one, and no mistake.'

Sir Lancelot glared. 'Perhaps it would be advantageous if I saw your principal?'

'I think it most certainly would.' She picked up one of the telephones. 'You happen to be in luck this morning. She's free. Usually clients have to wait up to a month. Hello! Mrs Hotblack, I've a gentleman here I think you'd better handle personally. Very well, Mrs Hotblack. First floor,' she added to Sir Lancelot.

He went up the stairs. He knocked and entered another small office, businesslike with unadorned green-painted walls and a row of heavy steel filing cabinets. Behind a well-tidied mahogany desk sat a woman about his own size. She was dressed in an expensive bottle-green silk suit, with brilliantly-tinted red hair and a monocle.

'Do sit down.'

She spoke in a low voice, without opening her mouth very much. He took the high-backed chair opposite the desk, balancing his homburg on his knee. She drew from a folder a long form covered with printed questions.

'First, your name.'

'Sir Lancelot Spratt.'

She looked up. 'Oh, a title?'

'There is still no law in the country against such indulgences.'

'Genuine, I suppose?'

Sir Lancelot bit his lip again. But he supposed if he wanted results in a hurry he'd better play their game, without too much sensitivity. 'I would have no objection to your telephoning the Palace to find out. Though possibly others might.'

Mrs Hotblack made a note. 'Occupation?'

'I am a surgeon.'

She looked with new interest through her monocle. 'That's curious.

117

We seldom see surgeons in here.'

'Surgeons need looking after like less adulated mortals.'

'Naturally. But medical men never seem to require our services.'

'Perhaps they are less particular than myself?'

'How very kind.'

Sir Lancelot scratched his beard. Everyone in the building was unbalanced, quite clearly. 'How long will it take you to fix me up?'

'You mean, simply to meet a suitable lady?'

'I mean to get the whole thing cut and dried. I'm an extremely busy man, you know. And a somewhat impatient one. I really can't carry on by myself any longer, or I shall burst an artery.'

'But surely you can wait a few days, at least?'

'I certainly can not.'

Mrs Hotblack gave him another close glance, shook her head, and turned back to the form. 'Single, divorced, or widower?'

'Widower. Though I fail to see what that has to do with it, in the least.'

'We are a very well-established, respectable and exclusive agency. We have to make exhaustive enquiries on both sides.'

'Things certainly weren't so strict when I first set up house with my late wife.'

'You found her through an agency, did you?'

'That remark was uncalled for, madam. I should not like anyone to give out that I married my housekeeper.'

'I must apologize,' she said quickly. 'I certainly didn't want to touch a sensitive spot. We take great care to avoid doing so, in fact.'

'I am not going to answer any more damnfool questions.' Sir Lancelot rose. 'I am a knight, a consultant surgeon at St Swithin's Hospital, and this card has my address. If you consider my moral character and worldly circumstances up to whatever standards you happen to have set yourself, kindly send a lady round to see me. If she dislikes the look of me, or me her, that will be the end of the matter.'

'At least you have a down-to-earth practical view of the process.' She couldn't suppress an admiring glance through the monocle.

'I am a down-to-earth practical man. Your fee will be paid in any case. Plus, of course, the female's travelling expenses.'

'I think that is being altogether too practical.'

'As you wish. I shall be at home all evening.'

Sir Lancelot stalked out. He noticed a telephone kiosk on the opposite pavement, and hurried across the road. He dialled the number of Frankie's London flat, but there was no reply. It was the second time he had called since leaving Dr Bonaccord's. He was anxious to have a little word with her.

20

In her white coat with stethoscope coiling from the pocket, a note-book under her arm, Muriel came into the students' common-room at St Swithin's from the wards that morning just before twelve-thirty. The long, dim ground-floor room, with its worn leather sofas, scratched tables, overcrowded notice-boards, and litter of newspapers, medical journals, sheets of case-notes and abandoned textbooks, though cleaned every morning always managed to look as untidy as a kindergarten. She noticed with satisfaction that the telephone booth in the corner was empty. Then she saw with less contentment her fiancé sitting beside it reading *Principles of Medicine*.

Edgar Sharpewhistle looked up. 'Hello, love.'

'Hello.'

'I was just thinking. Where do you want to go for your honeymoon?'

'Oh, anywhere.'

'Cornwall do you?'

'I don't mind.'

'Not much to do down there, of course. But if we're on honeymoon we'll be making our own fun, as it were, won't we?'

'Will we?'

'I mean, that's the point, isn't it?'

'What's the point?'

'Making fun. Together.'

'What *are* you talking about?'

'Bit of a rush, this wedding.' Sharpewhistle decided not to pursue the subject. 'There's my folk to come down from Pontefract. The best man to find. And I suppose you'll want some bridesmaids?' 'On the contrary, I should prefer to perform without an audience. We need only a couple of witnesses. I'd be perfectly happy with two passers-by from the street.'

'And where do you want to live?'

'Anywhere.'

'There's a two-room flat I heard of near my digs, behind the bus depot. It's a bit pricey, of course. But everywhere is.' He still had his index finger on his place in the textbook. 'Pity I can't move into your flat in Lazar Row, at least until the baby's born. Though I suppose you'll all be moving out, now your father's vice-chancellor of Hampton Wick.'

'He isn't. He turned it down.'

Sharpewhistle looked aghast. 'What did he do that for?'

'He felt too many people from St Swithin's would be after him for jobs.' The telephone rang. Sharpewhistle started to get up. 'It's for me,' she told him.

'But how do you know?'

'Extrasensory perception.'

Muriel went into the telephone box, closing the door. Sharpewhistle turned back to his *Principles of Medicine*. He became aware of someone in a white coat on the leather sofa beside him.

'And how's the happy groom?' asked Tulip Twyson.

'You know, do you?'

'Muriel told me. Though you're keeping it pretty dark in the hospital, I must say.'

'Muriel's a bit shy about these things.'

She decided to spare him her knowledge of his paternity. 'I must say, it came as a bit of a shock to me.'

'To me too, I suppose.'

'When did it all start?'

Sharpewhistle kept his finger on his place. 'The night of the May ball.'

'Pity I was already booked when you asked me first.'

'Yes, it was,' he said feelingly.

She laughed. 'The trouble with you, Edgar, is that you need someone to bring out the best in you.'

'You don't think Muriel would?'

'Well, did she?'

'How do you mean?'

'The night after the ball.'

'No, not really.' He moved awkwardly in his seat. 'I didn't think you were really much interested in me.'

'Oh, yes I was. It's delightful, isn't it, how one can be frank and open about everything now? The sex game is an awful bore, sometimes, however you play it. But I *was* interested in you, Edgar. Brains are sexy, you know. If you win this *IQ Quiz* thing, you could have almost any girl you wanted.'

Sharpewhistle looked interested. 'You think so?'

'You'd be irresistible. It's biological, isn't it? Pure Darwinism. A woman wants to mate with best-quality material. I was reading that every actress in London wanted to sleep with George Bernard Shaw, when he was a hundred and fifty years old and only ate nuts.'

'It's a bit late now, isn't it?' He looked at her complainingly. 'You should have told me all this before.'

'Can I come to the wedding?'

'No. But I can get you a seat for *IQ Quiz*.'

'That won't be half so entertaining, but I'll accept.'

'You'd better win, you know,' came a voice.

Sharpewhistle looked up. The tall, stylish figure of Roger Duckham was leaning over him. 'I can but do my best,' he said modestly.

'We all hope, for your own sake, that your best is going to be good enough.'

'You know, it's nice how all the boys in the medical school are encouraging me. I never thought I was so popular, honestly.'

Roger Duckham gave a chilling grin. 'We've not fallen in love with your big blue eyes, Sharpewhistle. We've got an absolute packet on you.'

He looked mystified. 'What sort of packet?'

'Money. Side-bets, of course. Mainly with those cowboys at High Cross. So your IQ had better be sizzling at the next round, hadn't it? If you let us down...it's the full treatment, my little man, take it from me. Do you remember, Tulip darling, that student a couple of years ago who let High Cross get away with our rugger mascot?'

'Oh, yes. The one we all gave the enema to.'

'What of?' asked Sharpewhistle faintly.

'Of Guinness.'

'There was something else in it, wasn't there?' asked Tulip.

'Turpentine and soft soap, as I remember offhand.'

'Then we hung him from the railings in the courtyard by his trousers.'

'I think it was then he saw the error of his ways. What did you say, Sharpewhistle?'

'I…I'll certainly cudgel my brains if it's for the good of the hospital.'

'You cudgel them, Sharpewhistle. You do that little thing.'

The telephone kiosk door opened. 'Sorry I can't stay, Edgar,' said Muriel, striding off. 'I've just remembered a blood-sugar I have to take in the wards.'

Outside the common-room was Sir Lancelot, walking along the main corridor, hands clasped behind his back, beard sunk on his chest. The sight of Muriel seemed to bring back the real world about him with a jerk. 'I believe I must congratulate you,' he said as jovially as possible. 'I gather you are shortly to be married.'

'Yes. That's right. Thanks.' She fell in beside him, walking towards the main entrance.

'Your father and myself had a chat about it last night, while we were taking a breath of air before retiring.'

'Poor Father.'

'Why so?'

'He's had so many worries lately.'

Sir Lancelot nodded sympathetically. 'But I'm sure a man of his intellectual fibre…of his moral strength…of his absolute refusal to shun any unpleasant duty…will take them all in his stride.'

'At least he hasn't got to be vice-chancellor at Hampton Wick.'

Sir Lancelot gave a slight, knowing smile. 'Where did you learn about the appointment? It's supposed to be a secret till Monday.'

'Oh, Father told us the day before yesterday. He'd had lunch with Dr Humble – she used to be his house-physician, but now she's an MP, of course – and she offered him the job. He was so dreadfully worried, and I don't blame him after all the terrible things the students do to their vice-chancellors there. The thought of him facing it made me feel quite sick. It isn't a job suitable for a man of intelligence, I'd say. They just want some big academic bully in to handle them. Anyway, thank God he got out of it. I don't know how, but he's been going round chortling at his cleverness all morning.' Sir Lancelot had stopped dead. His eyebrows were moving up and down and he had gone purple. 'I'm afraid I must go now, Uncle Lancelot. I've got to see someone off Piccadilly in half-an-hour. I'll tell Father how kind you were about him.'

She trotted away, peeling off her white coat, making towards the women students' cloakroom. Sir Lancelot stood opening and closing his fists. He turned and strode across the main hall, thrusting aside the plate-glass doors, pushing unseeing into the sunshine through startled students, nurses and patients. Hands jammed in jacket pockets, head down, he charged across the courtyard. He mowed his way through the shoppers in the main road, turned into Lazar Row, mounted the steps of No 2, put his finger on the bell and kept it there.

The dean had decided to lunch at home, and was just sitting down with his wife to a tasty-looking grilled sole with black butter and tomato. He put down his fish-knife and fork. 'That's odd – the bell's stuck. Never known it go wrong before.'

'These houses are really awfully badly made, dear.'

The dean went through to the hall. He opened the front door.

'You traitor!' shouted Sir Lancelot. 'You Judas! You rat!'

'Lancelot! Someone might overhear.'

'And a bloody good job, too. The more people who see you in your true colours the better. You false friend. You stabber in the back. You hypocrite. You slyboots.'

The dean grasped the situation. 'I suppose you got to know Frankie first offered the vice-chancellor's job to me?'

'And you got her to push it on me. Because you were too big a coward to take it yourself.'

'But I was doing you a favour, Lancelot. Be reasonable. You always wanted that job. Five years ago you behaved like a kid with no Christmas presents when you didn't get it.'

'That's beside the point. You deliberately deceived me on this very doorstep, barely twelve hours ago. You are no gentleman.'

'As usual, you're making far too much fuss about this. If I was Frankie's first choice for the job, what of it? You're jealous, that's all. A remarkably childish reaction, if I may say so.'

'Listen, cocky, don't flatter yourself. You weren't the first she offered the job to.' Sir Lancelot jerked a thumb. 'That was Bonaccord.'

'What? I can't believe that for one moment.'

'Then go and ask his secretary. She made a point of telling me as much this morning.'

'That's absolutely outrageous of Frankie. She let me understand most definitely that I was her very first choice. How a woman like her could for one moment envisage a wet like Bonaccord in the job, and then go to him ahead of me...why, she must have been out of her mind.'

Sir Lancelot smirked. 'Jealousy is a remarkably childish reaction.'

'I'm not jealous. Not at all. Me? Of Bonaccord? Don't be ridiculous. Anyway, what are you going to do about it?'

'Tell Frankie she can put her job where Cromwell told them to put the Mace.'

The dean began to recover himself. 'If you'll excuse me, I shall continue with my luncheon. My fish will be getting cold.'

'I never want to speak to you again, Lychfield.'

'I can assure you the opportunity will never arise, Spratt.'

The dean shut the door.

'What's the matter?' asked Josephine in alarm.

'Oh, it was Lancelot. Frankie Humble's made a fool of us both. I'm sorry, dear,' he added quickly, sitting down. 'I know it distresses you when I mention her name.'

'But why should it, Lionel? We've known Frankie for years, and I'm very fond of her. I think the more you see of her the better. It livens you up.'

The dean stared at her for a moment, but decided to make no

comment. Instead, he said, 'Do you mind if I get on with my fish in silence, dear? I have a little work to get through before my clinic this afternoon.'

He drew from his pocket four sheets of foolscap paper. He scored with heavy strokes through alterations made that very morning. After a moment's thought, he substituted, *His testiness, his egotism and his jealousy of his colleagues during his final years assumed such proportions that they were obliged to watch helplessly the ultimate demolition of the splendid ruin he had already become.*

Next door, Sir Lancelot was sitting down at his study desk, uncapping his fountain-pen, and squaring his shoulders.

21

'Officer,' said Sir Lancelot. 'I wish to see Dr Frances Humble. She works here.'

'Queue for the public gallery over there, sir,' said the policeman.

'I do not wish to sit in the public gallery. I wish to go inside and speak to Dr Humble.'

'Just take your place in the queue, sir. You'll get a seat all right before the House rises.'

Big Ben overhead boomed ten o'clock. It was the same evening, warm, starlit and airless.

'I happen to know that Dr Humble is inside the House of Commons. I saw as much in the evening paper. She is engaged in debating the new Education Bill. It is a matter of the utmost public importance that I should see her.'

'I'm afraid everyone has to queue for the public gallery, sir.'

Sir Lancelot held a hand before his eyes. 'I wish to lobby my MP.'

'Have you a ticket, sir?'

'I am demanding to exercise the sacred right of a free-born Englishman.'

'Still got to have a ticket, sir.'

'Good God, officer! Is this democracy?'

'Come along, sir, No offensive language, please.'

'Can't I even send in a message?'

'Queue for the public gallery over there, sir.'

The policeman turned to assist a party of tourists looking for the Post Office Tower. Sir Lancelot stood wondering what to do next. He had telephoned Frankie half a dozen times since lunch without success. To be conscripted by her as second-best to Bonaccord was bad enough. But second-best to the dean was unthinkable. He was determined to fling her perfidy in her face before he went to bed. Besides, there was no time to waste, if she were to find yet another vice-chancellor. He looked round wildly. It was unfortunate that the House of Commons, of all edifices in the country, should be purpose-built to keep out the unwelcome. He had half-resigned himself to defeat, when Frankie herself came down the steps from the arched, carved doors, talking earnestly to a man of schoolmasterish appearance.

'Frankie! I must see you this instant.'

She looked up and smiled. She bade her visitor farewell, and crossed to Sir Lancelot. 'Why on earth are you standing there mixed with the populace? I could have given you a ticket, had you wanted to hear the debate.'

'I do not wish to hear any debate. Nor shall there be any on what I am about to say. That vice-chancellor's job at Hampton Wick. I withdraw my application.'

'A little sudden, isn't it?'

'No more sudden than the blow of my discovering you offered it first to Lychfield, and even before him to Bonaccord.'

'I can't see why you should make a fuss. Even Ministers of the Crown aren't above accepting an office turned down by others.'

'But you led me to believe, Frankie, that I was your first choice. I accepted on those terms. I am very, very hurt.'

'Poor Lancelot,' she said with deep sympathy.

'And you were very, very naughty.'

'Perhaps I was. But politics is a very, very naughty business.'

'So you'll have to find someone else.'

'Oh, no I won't. I've had enough trouble filling this job already.'

'I shall refuse to accept it.'

'Aren't you being a little silly?' Sir Lancelot saw her nose twitch. But at that moment he was twitchproof. 'The official announcement's already typed, and probably issued to the press. They'll have a lot of questions to ask if you simply disown it. Why you've got cold feet, for a start.'

'I shall say you tricked me into it.'

'Very well. That I tricked you while alone with you, in your house one night. While my husband was away. If you want to present me in that sort of light to my constituents and the rest of the public, you are quite entitled to. But I'm afraid that my political friends would see that it was the end of your career, too.'

Sir Lancelot looked shocked. 'Frankie, surely you don't really think I would be capable of such conduct? Especially with you. After all, there are limits.'

She gave him a sweet smile. 'Of course, you'd never even think of it. You're far too gallant, in such a lovely old-fashioned way.'

'Then you'll voluntarily withdraw your offer?'

'No. So there's not much you can do about it, really, is there? Now I must get back to the Chamber. There's such a boring little man on his feet, but I know he always treats himself to exactly forty minutes of everybody's time.'

Frankie hurried back up the steps, the policeman saluting. Sir Lancelot made to follow.

'Queue for the public gallery over there, sir.'

'It is essential that I speak to that lady.'

'Come along, sir. Even the Queen herself isn't allowed in where she's going.'

Sir Lancelot glowered. But five hundred years of privilege wrung in words and blood stood impenetrably between him and his quarry. 'In which case, officer, perhaps you would kindly direct me to a telephone box instead?'

'Corner of Parliament Square, sir.'

The box was empty. Sir Lancelot felt for a coin, and dialled. There was some delay before anyone answered.

'Bonaccord? Spratt here. I understand that a few days ago you were honoured with an offer of the vice-chancellorship of Hampton Wick University.'

'That is perfectly true.'

'I am asking with the full authority of Dr Frances Humble that you reconsider your decision, and that you take it.'

'That's out of the question.'

'Why? A nut-wallah like you is just what they want.'

'I should prefer to continue with clinical work, thank you very much.'

'You haven't the guts, that's what.'

'Fortunately I am not given to crude emotions, Lancelot. But were I a man of uncontrolled instinct I should find that remark most offensive.'

Sir Lancelot swallowed. 'I apologize. I apologize slavishly.' His voice took on an oily sheen. 'Paradoxically enough, my language was dictated solely by regard for your splendid qualities. I was merely trying to goad you into taking the job, for the benefit of the university and all concerned.'

'But I'm not at all the right type. They want some thick-skinned red-necked old academic hack who'll simply put up with them. The entire Institute of Psychiatry couldn't tame those students.'

Dr Bonaccord realized he was talking to himself. He raised his eyebrows, and put back the hall telephone with a sigh. He was in stockinged feet, trousers and mauve-striped shirt open to the waist. He went back to the bedroom.

'Who was it?'

'That stupid old bleeder Spratt.'

'What did he want? Something about Miss MacNish?'

'No, he seems to have got wind of my being offered the Hampton Wick job.'

Gisela bit the end of one finger guiltily. 'That was me, I'm afraid.'

'It doesn't matter. For some reason he was pressing me to take it. I suppose it's been offered to someone else whose insides he hates even more than my own. You do look attractive like that.'

'Flatterer.'

'Turn in your toes and put your knees together. That's right. Do your naughty little schoolgirl.'

'Like that? Aren't you glad I kept my old school clothes?'

He lay full length on the bed. 'Mmmmm…'

'Though it's a bore having to hide them locked away in the desk. I don't know what Miss MacNish would say if she found a gym-slip and striped tie.'

'And a badge saying "House Prefect".' Gisela smiled, inspecting herself in the long mirror. 'They still fit. A bit tight in the bust, that's all.'

'The straw boater is a lovely touch.'

'Do you like it?' she asked eagerly.

'Especially on the back of your head.'

She rearranged it. 'Remember when you used to wait to carry my books home from school?'

He laughed softly. 'And nobody here even suspects we knew each other then.'

'It was so far away in the country.'

'And before you'd met your husband.'

They laughed together. Gisela sprang lightly on to the white-covered bed where he lay relaxed, arms behind his head, She started delicately tickling his left ear with the toe of her black school stocking.

'Nice?'

He nodded. 'What do you most admire about me?'

'That's a very difficult one.'

'Try.'

'Well, you're very clever.'

'Yes. I am. And I'm different from others. I understand the human mind. I understand my own mind. I am clean of the prejudices, hates, idiocies, obsessions and phobias of ordinary mortals. I am normal. That is a tremendous achievement.'

'Of course it is, Cedric.' She spoke gently and admiringly.

He reached out and picked up a grubby white tennis shoe. 'It's got your name inside it.'

'It's the pair I used to wear for games.'

He put it under his nose, savouring it like a highly-bred rose. The doorbell rang.

'Bloody hell!' Dr Bonaccord got off the bed. He slipped on a short dressing-gown, went down to the hall and opened the front door. Outside was a tall, thin middle-aged lady in a wide-brimmed hat, carrying a small suitcase.

'Sir Lancelot Sprite?' she asked.

'This is the wrong number. Sir Lancelot is at No. 3.'

'Oh? I was ringing there for a quite considerable time.' She had the sort of voice heard announcing the prizes at suburban fetes. 'So I imagined I was mistaken.'

'I'm afraid I can't help you,' he said shortly. 'Is it urgent? Are you a patient?'

'I am in no need of medical attention, thank you. I shall have to hang about until he returns. Though I am not in the least used to hanging about, I can assure you.'

The psychiatrist shut the door. His visitor walked up and down Lazar Row, looking petulant. But it was not long before a taxi drew up before No 3 and a stout man with a beard got out. She assumed a smile, approaching from the shadows. 'Sir Lancelot Sprite?'

'Spratt's the name. Who are you?'

'I am Mrs Grimley. I am here through the agency of Hotblack's.'

'Thank God you've turned up. Come inside.'

He switched on the light in the hall. 'Charming place,' she said, following him.

'Glad you like it. Through here is my sitting-room.' Sir Lancelot paused. He rubbed his hands briskly. 'You must forgive me, madam, but I have just endured one of the most trying days of my life. Would you object if I had a whisky and soda?'

'But not at all. I always believe a man is entitled to his tipple.'

'Er…perhaps you'd join me, Mrs Grimley?' he asked politely.

'Thank you. Ever so. I would be quite partial to a small one.'

Sir Lancelot produced two crystal tumblers and a bottle of Glenlivet. 'Say when.' He poured the spirit. 'Say when.' He poured some more. 'Say when.'

'It does so restore the morale, don't you think?'

'Say when.'

'Oh! I wasn't noticing.'

'Soda or water?'

'I'll take it straight, thank you ever so. Mud in your eye.'

Sir Lancelot poured his own drink. 'I suppose you're pretty experienced?'

'Well… I *am* a widow.'

'H'm. As you may have gathered from Hotblack's, I am a widower.'

'*And* a knight. I'm very thrilled, I must say.'

'It is hardly the most magnificent of distinctions. Or perhaps one just gets used to it, like one's cricket colours at school.'

'I don't think I'd *ever* get used to calling myself "Lady Spratt".'

'No? Perhaps my late wife didn't. Where are you from, Mrs Grimley?'

'Wiveliscombe. That's in Somerset, you know.'

'You've had a long journey.'

'Too, too exhausting! Do you think I could restore myself with another little drinkey?'

'Yes, of course.' Sir Lancelot looked at her doubtfully. 'Do you…er, shift much of this stuff?'

'In strictest moderation, I assure you. Except when I'm tired. My poor late husband passed away with it. Chin-chin.'

He sat in the armchair, sticking out his legs. 'Do sit down, Mrs Grimley. I don't insist on formality here, you know. I hope you'll decide to stay.'

She took the straight-backed chair opposite, crossing her legs and modestly tugging the hem of her skirt, holding her glass with both hands on her knees. 'How very kind.'

'I've been without anyone now for two days.'

She gave a shriek. 'Your wife! She's only just died? Not even buried?'

'No, no, no. I had someone living here to look after me. A housekeeper.'

'A *housekeeper*!' She giggled and winked.

'Hotblack's must have explained to you that I suggested we took a look at each other. If we both approved, we'd go ahead without any more fuss and bother.' She nodded. 'For my part, Mrs Grimley, I should be delighted to take you on.'

'Oh! Sir Lancelot.' She dropped her eyes.

'And for your part?'

'You have made me the happiest woman in London.'

'H'm. Well. That's settled then.'

'Might I have another wee one? It's all so trying on the nerves.' She picked up the bottle and helped herself.

'When can you start? Tonight?'

'Oh! You are impatient.' She closed her eyes appreciatively. 'Quite a bull pawing the ground, a stallion champing at the bit.'

'I told you, I've had no one for two days. It'll be a great relief, I make no secret of it.'

'I am yours to command,' she said grandly.

'Good. Well, first you'll have to go up to the bedroom and make the bed.' She stood up and aimed for the door, swaying hardly perceptibly. 'By the way, I don't know if Hotblack's charge you anything. But I'll send them a cheque to cover both of our fees in the morning.'

She turned round and gently patted his face. 'How sweet you are. But I'm afraid my fees are rather on the large side, because I have been on their books for quite a wee time, you know. Still, what's it matter if they deliver the goods in the end? To think! I was actually on the point of losing faith in any matrimonial agency at all.'

22

'I wonder who the woman was I saw going into Lancelot's house?' asked Josephine in the sitting-room of No 2.

The dean looked up quickly from his *Proceedings of the Royal Society of Medicine*. 'It wasn't Frankie?'

'Oh no, dear, I'd always recognize Frankie. It was someone very strange. She looked as though they'd forgotten to tidy her away after the Chelsea Flower Show.'

'I wouldn't be surprised at any company Lancelot keeps. He's really a disgrace to the neighbourhood. He goes round shouting his head off, he crashes about in there half the night, and he reeks of onions. I wish to God he'd move out.'

'That isn't very charitable of you, Lionel.'

'Charitable? Lancelot's about as deserving of charity as a successful bank robber.'

'Daddy, do shut up,' said Muriel, not lifting her eyes from her *Lancet*.

'Kindly do not speak to me like that,' said the dean icily.

'You're always carrying on about Uncle Lancelot. It bores me.'

'Just because you're going to be a married woman doesn't mean you can irritate your parents with a display of condescension.'

'Lionel! Remember her condition.'

The dean snorted.

'If you ask me –' began Edgar Sharpewhistle, a finger keeping his place in the *Journal of Hospital Medicine*.

'For God's sake, don't you start,' said the dean. They were enjoying a family evening. Muriel had to the dean's annoyance insisted strongly on her fiancé being asked for dinner, and then made a point of their all sitting together over the coffee.

'After all,' she had claimed. 'We've got to get used to each other's company some time, haven't we?'

Sharpewhistle started looking anxiously round for the brandy, but the dean had hidden it. Suddenly Muriel stood up.

'Ah! You're both off,' said the dean.

'Father. The time is just on ten-thirty. A crisis is about to arise in my life,' Sharpewhistle blinked.

'Now, now, dear,' said Josephine. 'You're being a little emotional. It's only to be expected in your delicate state.'

Muriel glanced at her watch. 'At any moment someone will walk through the front door to change the lives of all of us.'

'What *are* you raving about?' complained the dean. 'Who do you expect at this hour? It's hardly the season for Santa Claus.'

'I wanted you, Father, and Mother – and you, Edgar – to be here when he arrived. That's why I engineered the dinner-party. He couldn't come earlier because of his job.'

'Love, you've been overworking,' suggested Sharpewhistle.

'Muriel, my dear,' said the dean. 'Possibly you're in the grip of some hallucination or other. How about the pair of us slipping next door to Bonaccord?'

The doorbell rang. They all looked at one another. 'I'll go,' said Muriel.

She reappeared with a tall, thin, pale, clean but shabbily-dressed young man.

'Mother... Father... Edgar...this is Andrew Clarke.'

The dean jumped up and glared. 'And what, may I ask, do you want?'

'I want to marry your daughter.'

'Good God,' muttered the dean. 'It's me. Yes, I'm the patient. I've developed organized delusions. Probably schizophrenia. Must see Bonaccord at once.'

'Here, steady on – ' began Edgar.

'Oh, Andy,' said Muriel. 'This is my fiancé.'

Andy extended his hand. 'Peace to you, my friend. Hold no rancour in your heart, I pray you.'

'You're pulling my bird—'

'Life is such a magnificent gift, brother,' he continued, 'our destinies so mysterious, we cannot let our vision be clouded by trivialities.'

'You can't just pinch my wife—'

'Peace, peace—'

'I'd give you a punch on the nose, if I was bigger.'

'Edgar, do please avoid making an exhibition of yourself.'

'Anyway, I feel quite sick.'

'Who is this man?' demanded the dean. 'Where did you bring him from?'

'I have known Andy for some months, Father. Since I was doing my sociology course. We are very much in love with one another.'

'Sociology student, is he? I might have known as much. Depraved, the lot of them.'

'No, Andy isn't one of the students. He's one of the subjects. He doesn't believe in money or possessions, or anything but leading a pure life. Though now he's got a steady job, you may like to know. So we want to get married.'

'An evening job, sir,' Andy explained. 'Washing up in a hotel. It's remarkable the satisfaction one can get from scraping dirty plates.'

The dean wagged his finger. 'Don't imagine that you're going to get any financial assistance from me. Not a penny, I assure you. Nor are you going to move in and live here, free of charge...' He stopped. He stared at Sharpewhistle and Andy in turn, then finally at Muriel. He added in a weak voice, 'Er...does he...your new young man...*know*?'

'I'm aware, sir, that Muriel is expecting a child by another man.' He bowed courteously towards Sharpewhistle. 'But that is a mere nothing, compared with our own future happiness.'

'You mean you're...you're prepared to rear this cuckoo?'

'It will be Muriel's child.'

'Here! What about me?' demanded Sharpewhistle.

'Do be quiet, Edgar. You must try and adjust yourself like an adult.'

'But I'm the father of it! Don't I count at all?'

'Yes, it *must* be mass delusions,' muttered the dean. 'First thing tomorrow morning, we'll all five of us have to go and see Bonaccord.'

'You've got to marry me,' shouted Sharpewhistle.

'Nothing in this world would make me do that, Edgar. I must have been mad to contemplate it in the first place.'

'Well, that's all very satisfactory, isn't it?' Josephine spoke for the first time. 'Muriel will marry Andy, whom she is very fond of and the baby will have a nice, cheerful home. It's a little hard on you, Edgar, I must admit, but I'm sure you'll take it in a very reasonable way. After all, there're plenty of other very nice girls about the place, whom you can make pregnant in the fullness of time.'

'Drugs!' exclaimed the dean. 'I've got it! That's what you're on, young man, aren't you? Hallucinogens. The obvious diagnosis.'

'I take neither drugs, sir, nor tobacco, nor alcohol nor meat. My life is devoted to purity, to sweetness towards others, and to intellectual integrity.'

Sharpewhistle stood in the corner making choking noises. Josephine continued calmly, 'As everything's settled, Lionel, why not get that bottle of champagne from the fridge to celebrate?'

'What's the point, my dear, he says he doesn't drink alcohol... I mean, the whole thing is outrageous. Ridiculous. Impossible. I won't hear a single word of it. Muriel! Come to your senses. You must marry young Sharpewhistle there.'

'I refuse to.'

'Why couldn't you get this other fellow to put you in the family way in the first place?' asked the dean furiously. 'Why do you have to make life so bloody complicated for all of us? Absolutely typical of a female medical student!'

There was a crash. An iron casserole came sailing through the window. Josephine screamed. The dean stared through the shattered glass in horror. 'Send for the police. Dial 999 instantly.'

'Let me in,' shouted Sir Lancelot from the pavement. 'I'm being raped.'

'Come back, you old sod.' A shrill female voice rang from outside. 'You're not going to walk out on me like this, you randy old doctor –'

'Madam! Will you please desist in hurling household appliances at me?'

'Are you coming to bed or aren't you?'

'You are to leave my premises at once.'

'What, at this time of night? You must be joking. Go all the way back to

Wiveliscombe? That's your game, is it? Lead me on and throw me out. Like this, too, with hardly a stitch on my back.'

'Muriel dear, I think it would be convenient for Sir Lancelot if you opened the front door,' said Josephine.

The surgeon staggered into the room, wiping his face with his red-spotted handkerchief. The dean perched on the edge of the sofa, staring into the middle distance and biting his nails.

'And who *was* your friend, Lancelot?' asked Josephine.

'A middle-aged alcoholic nymphomaniac.'

Josephine looked through the broken window. 'She seems to have retreated inside your house. I expect in that state she found the night air chilly.'

'You may possibly be wondering how in the name of God I managed to get mixed up with her?'

'Don't think I'm nosy, Lancelot, but it would seem of interest.'

'I went to a place called Hotblack's – '

'Lancelot! So you decided to marry again, after all? How charming.'

'No, I did not blasted well decide to get married. Nor shall I. Nor have another female of any description whatever in my house again. I imagined Hotblack's was a domestic employment agency.'

'Oh, dear. You should have gone to Morpeth's in the Strand. I'll telephone them tomorrow. Though perhaps it would be best if I asked them to send the ladies to be interviewed at St Swithin's?'

Sir Lancelot sat down heavily next to the dean.

'Couldn't you have simply thrown her out?' asked Josephine.

'She said she liked the brutal approach. When she appeared, I thought she was at least civilized. Quite refined, in fact. She was raising her elbow rather, though I was prepared to put that down to nerves. In the end, she turned out a…a monster. I only hope I can get rid of her somehow tomorrow. I see I owe you for a window.'

'But where are you going to sleep?'

'It is totally out of the question to return to my own house, of course. I rather hoped, Josephine, that I could impose on you for a shakedown here?'

'That would be no trouble, honestly.'

'This sofa would suit me perfectly well.'

She looked doubtful. 'You're sure you'd be comfortable enough?'

'Mother –'

Sir Lancelot looked up. He seemed to see the three others for the first time.

'Yes, dear?'

'I'm afraid Andy will have to stay here the night, too.'

'Of course he can. But he hasn't brought any things, has he?'

'My things,' said Andy with a saintly gesture, 'are in my pockets. A man should never own more possessions than he can carry on his person.'

'If he stays, I stay.' Sharpewhistle stared angrily at everybody. 'To see there isn't any hanky-panky.'

'Oh, dear, that might make the house a little crowded.'

'But Andy's got nowhere else to go, Mother. Usually, he sleeps where they put the hotel garbage, but they will have locked it up by now.'

'How very awkward. Well, Andy, if you would care to sleep down here on the sofa, and if Edgar will sleep in the spare room on the first floor, then I'll move into the divan bed in your room on the top, Muriel. And Sir Lancelot can share our own bedroom with Lionel.'

The dean came to life. 'I utterly refuse.'

'Now you're being churlish, Lionel.'

'I will not sleep in the same room as Lancelot. It strikes me as quite unhygienic.'

'Well, you'd better share the sofa down here with young Andy, then.' The dean jumped up. He pulled half a dozen copies of *The Medical Annual* out of the bookcase, and removed the bottle of brandy lying on its side behind them. 'So *that's* where you'd hidden it,' said Josephine. 'I do wish I'd known after dinner.'

'I am taking this liqueur cognac up to our bedroom. I am going to drink as much as possible before it anaesthetizes me. I shall then not care in the least if my bedmate is to be Lancelot, Andy, Edgar or all three. And the lady next door, too, if she feels like it.'

He marched from the room, Sir Lancelot following. The dean went straight through his bedroom to the bathroom, produced a tooth-mug, and half-filled it with brandy.

'I say, dean,' murmured Sir Lancelot. 'I could do with a peg of that.'

For a second the dean glared, but relented. He fetched Josephine's tooth-mug, gurgled in the brandy, and handed it over in silence. The pair sat on the twin beds.

'We have problems,' observed Sir Lancelot.

The dean gulped his brandy and snorted. 'I have problems. My daughter having got herself pregnant by that over-moustached dwarf Sharpewhistle, now announces she wants to marry that El Greco leftover Andy, or whatever his name is.'

Sir Lancelot raised his eyebrows. 'You mean the fellow who sleeps on garbage? An odd situation, I must say. Ibsen might have made something of it.'

'My daughter is an odd female.' The dean took another gulp. 'She takes after her mother.'

'While *I* am let in for this bloody vice-chancellor's job.' Sir Lancelot half-drained the brandy. 'Did you see the Hampton Wick students' latest antics?' he asked gloomily. 'They got bored with hanging their professors in effigy –'

'I should imagine so. They're always up to it.'

'So they decided to do it for real. I believe the poor fellow escaped with a stiff neck and a severe fright. He was the Professor of Criminology, too.'

The dean winced. 'If only we could get Bonaccord to accept, after all. I wouldn't worry very much if they hanged him. Nor drew and quartered him while they were at it.'

'He's already told me he won't.'

'Can't we put some pressure on him?'

'What pressure? We can hardly blackmail him. He's perfectly open about his fornication with that girl, and doesn't give a damn anyway.'

'But at his age, the vice-chancellorship of Hampton Wick would be a big step in his career. Can't he take a rational view?'

'Rational? Don't be stupid. He's a psychiatrist.' There was a silence. 'It's all Frankie's fault.'

The dean nodded. 'I'm afraid it is.'

'It was moreover Frankie who sent me to the marriage agency instead of the domestic agency.' For the first time, the dean laughed. Sir Lancelot looked at him bleakly. 'I fail to see anything funny in it, dean. Frankie simply took us both for a ride. She doubtless looks upon us as a pair of burbling old fools.'

'You know, Lancelot, I'm beginning to believe something which I have long suspected. Frankie's a bitch.'

'I'm inclined to agree with you, dean.'

The dean yawned. 'We'd better get some sleep, I suppose. You're examining in surgery tomorrow, aren't you?'

Sir Lancelot nodded.

'It's the finals of the Royal Society of Bleeders.'

'At least that won't be very exacting on the brain. I expect you'd care to borrow a pair of my pyjamas?'

'Don't be ridiculous. I'd look like a hippopotamus in a zebra skin.'

When Sir Lancelot lay in the nude between Josephine's sheets, he said, 'Lionel…with Frankie…to be honest, now. Did you?'

'To be honest, Lancelot, no.'

'You don't mind my asking?'

'Not a bit.' There was a pause. 'And did you – to be perfectly honest?'

'To be perfectly and absolutely honest – no.'

'Remind me in the morning, Lancelot, to do a little work at some writing I have in my desk.'

'And perhaps you'd remind me of some editing I must do on a literary effort in my own desk?'

'Of course, Lancelot. Good night.'

'Good night, Lionel.'

The dean switched out the light. For a long time he stared through the darkness at the ceiling, grappling with his troubles. But in a second Sir Lancelot was asleep and snoring, as usual.

23

Just before ten-thirty the following morning, the dean hurried in his bowler hat up the front steps of the wide granite entrance of the Old Bailey. He stood for a moment in the entrance-hall, looking confusedly at the barristers, policemen and, he supposed, criminals milling about. Then spotting a helmetless young constable sitting in a booth, he asked, 'Mr Humphrey Fletcher-Boote, please?' adding for full measure, 'QC'.

'I imagine you'd find him in the barristers' robing room, sir.'

'He said he'd come out here to collect me.'

'Are you his client, sir?'

'Oh, no,' exclaimed the dean. 'At least, not yet.'

'Lionel, there you are! My dear, dear fellow! What an unexpected pleasure.'

The deep voice which with commendable fairness had boomed blackly of the misdeeds of criminals, or alternately mellifluously indicated their innocence, which had humbly submitted to the wisdom of judges or passionately stirred the wits of juries, came ringing across the busy hall. Mr Fletcher-Boote was a big, red-faced cheerful man, in bands, wig and gown, advancing with huge hand outstretched.

'I hope you didn't mind my telephoning you at home so early?' the dean apologized.

'Not a bit. Delighted I could fit you in this morning. By jove, you're looking well.'

'Thank you. Though I didn't sleep a wink last night.'

The QC dug him hard in the ribs. 'Can't you doctors knock yourselves flat with drugs?' He gave another dig. 'Or do you simply count sheep like everyone else? How's the family? How's that clever young daughter of yours? She must be quite grown up now.'

'Grown up!' muttered the dean.

'We really must get a little golf, some time. Though I've honestly hardly touched a club since our days at the university. What's the bother?' he asked, noticing the clock and coming briskly to business.

'I wondered if I could cadge a little professional advice?'

'In trouble, eh?' The QC laughed heartily and dug the dean in the ribs again. 'General Medical Council, I suppose? Being naughty with the ladies, eh, Lionel? Just like you used to be.'

'It's entirely theoretical.' The dean looked deeply uncomfortable. 'You see... I, well, I'm examining students today. For the qualifying examination of the Royal Society of Bleeders – it has an ancient right to bestow medical degrees, you may know.'

'And it keeps a splendid cellar. I've dined there.'

'Doubtless. I wanted to ask questions more unusual than the general run – I'm afraid the Bleeders candidates do turn up time and time again, poor fellows, and I fancy only pass in the end because they've answered everything we can possibly ask. You know the medico-legal line –'

'Murder, rape and bestiality? All very interesting.'

'Something a little more esoteric, I thought. Now there's this girl –'

'Which girl?'

'Muriel.'

The QC frowned. 'That's the name of your daughter, isn't it?'

'Oh, she's got nothing to do with it. Nothing whatever. But I thought I'd better call this girl something, instead of just calling her "this girl". So I called her Muriel.'

'I see.'

'This girl – let's call her Mary instead – she's pregnant, you see.'

'Ah! A condition with almost limitless medicolegal possibilities – either after, or immediately before, its initiation.'

'Quite. Well, Muriel. That is, Mary. This girl. She's pregnant. By a man.'

'That would be hardly astounding.'

'No. Of course not. I meant, by this man, whom she knows.'

'Some girls don't know, of course. Dance halls in the provinces,' he added with a professional appreciation. 'How confused they can get in the dark afterwards.'

'But Muriel knows. This girl knows.'

'That's Mary?'

'She knows who did it.'

'She wants a bastardy order?'

'Not a bit. He's perfectly prepared to marry her.'

'Stout fellow.'

'But she doesn't want to marry him.'

'That's not unknown. After all, one may enjoyably sip a good port, but feel disinclined to lay down a whole cellarful.'

'She wants to marry somebody else.'

'The same girl?'

'Yes. Muriel. I mean, the pregnant girl.'

'Someone had better tell the other fellow pretty damn quick he's buying her in foal.'

'He knows.'

'And he's still prepared to marry her?'

'Yes.'

'Bloody fool.'

'He sleeps among the garbage.'

'So I should imagine. But you're making this story rather complicated for your exam candidates, aren't you?'

'What I'm trying to get down to, is simply this. Who is the father of the child?'

'The man who rodgered her, of course.'

'But who would legally be its father if the girl married the second chap?'

'The second chap.'

'But what about the first chap? Wouldn't he come into it?'

'The law always assumes any child born to a married couple is theirs. A bit hard on the husband sometimes, quite possibly. But you must agree it's a nice and tidy arrangement.'

'But –' The dean wagged a finger. 'Surely the girl wouldn't be allowed to marry the *second* chap if she was pregnant by the *first* chap? It would be…' He searched his mind for legal terms. 'Consanguinity.'

'That's nothing whatever to do with it.' Mr Fletcher-Boote looked offended at this assumption of legal knowledge. 'They could be married in Canterbury Cathedral by the Archbishop. It would be perfectly in order, as long as they could pay for the choir.'

'That strikes me as being utterly ridiculous.'

'Oh, I don't know. *Caveat emptor*, and so on. It's a man's own fault if he buys a pig in a poke. Or should I say a poked pig?' He laughed loudly, digging the dean in the ribs again. 'Of course, such a marriage would be voidable. It could be annulled by the courts, if certain conditions were observed, such as instituting the nullity proceedings within a year of the ceremony.'

'In that case, the marriage would be a marriage which never was?' asked the dean hopefully.

'Exactly. Void *ab initio*.'

'That might be a ray of hope.'

'Though of course, if the second chap – the chap who sleeps with the garbage – knew the girl was preggers when he went ahead and married her…well, that's the end of it. Unless he can show he was ignorant of the facts at the time, the marriage simply has to stand.'

The dean bit the rim of his bowler thoughtfully. 'But Andy is not at all ignorant of the facts.'

'Who's Andy?'

'Oh, no one…so I can't stop it? I mean – in this purely theoretical case – the marriage can go ahead? It can't even be disallowed afterwards?'

'I'd advise the couple to seek a divorce later, if they want to. Divorce has been made so simple and convenient one feels quite ashamed at pocketing the fees sometimes. Now I must go, Lionel. I am defending a financial gentleman, whose talents I fear are shortly to be lost to the City of London for some considerable time.'

The dean hurried away, looking anxiously at his watch. He should have been at St Swithin's, but he had telephoned his registrar to take his ward-round. He had strong views on shirkers but the crisis of a lifetime excused anything – even drinking brandy in the bedroom.

The others were waiting for him in the downstairs room at No 2 Lazar Row. Muriel was still reading the *Lancet*. Edgar Sharpewhistle was glaring silently at Andy, who with his eyes shut and his hands clasped seemed to be meditating. Josephine was sitting with a collander, shelling peas for lunch. None of them seemed to have spoken for some time.

The dean strode in, taking off his hat with a flourish. 'Well, I have taken advice, as I promised. Legal advice. The very best advice. Mr Fletcher-Boote, a most eminent QC. I was privileged to be given a consultation at short notice. I put the facts to him. I think I may say that I did so cogently, lucidly, with neither elaboration nor emotion – '

'Can I marry Andy or can't I?' asked Muriel impatiently.

'Yes.'

Andy opened his eyes. 'Bless him, bless him. Bless you, sir. Bless us all.' Muriel grabbed his arm and kissed him.

'Here, where do I come into this?' Sharpewhistle looked crosser than ever.

'Please be quiet, Edgar,' said the dean severely. 'The legal position is perfectly clear. You can marry Andy, Muriel, despite your...er, condition caught from Edgar. So far so good. I shall, however, disown you.'

'Lionel, you are old-fashioned. Children aren't chattels any more,' murmured Josephine. 'Ugh, maggots.'

'They may take my views how they like, my dear. They have invoked my displeasure. Doubtless that gives pain only to myself, not to Muriel. I think she is mad to marry this...this mystic dishwasher. Though I suppose if it *had* been illegal,' he added, ruefully, glancing at Sharpewhistle, 'we shouldn't be all that better off, back at square one.'

'I don't think I like that remark,' said Sharpewhistle.

'Please don't keep interrupting. I have suffered enough this morning already. To be quite frank, I should be happier at Muriel marrying you, Andy. She obviously loves you – I presume, possibly too generously, she's old enough and sensible enough to know her own feelings. And you are...er, quite tall, and I suppose personable – '

Sharpewhistle jumped up. 'I don't care for your tone – '

'Shut up. I am simply ashamed, bitterly ashamed, that she has decided to do so in such bizarre, indeed perverted, circumstances. Moreover, you are a hopeless drifter, a wastrel – '

'Sir. Bless you. May I say I am starting a regular job on Monday, to support my bride?'

'*Head* dishwasher, I presume?'

'No, sir. Research into the molecular structure of non-ferrous metals at temperatures approaching absolute zero.'

'I beg your pardon?'

'Andy got a double first,' Muriel explained. 'At Cambridge.'

'Where…where are you going to do all this, may I ask?' The dean looked even more bemused.

'In the research laboratories of Megaelectronics Limited, sir. My father is a director.'

'Well, of course this is completely different,' said the dean, rubbing his hands briskly.

'Here – !' said Sharpewhistle.

'Oh, do shut up.'

'I had rejected society, sir. But Muriel insists I cohere again. And I think she is right. With her personality behind me –'

'But of course, there's still this bloody baby,' muttered the dean.

'Oh, Father.' Muriel had been standing biting her knuckle. 'Excuse me a minute, will you? I must fetch something from my room.'

24

'Morning, George.' In his black jacket and striped trousers, rubbing his hands expectantly, Sir Lancelot came briskly through some specially arranged white cloth screens at one end of Virtue Ward in St Swithin's. 'Sorry I'm late. Had to spend a couple of hours this morning packing an ancient female relative back to Somerset. Gone now, thank God.'

'They can be a bore, these old dears.' His fellow examiner was from High Cross Hospital, a silver-haired surgeon in a dark suit and a lilac waistcoat with brass buttons. He put down his copy of The Angling Times. 'Been on the river much this season?'

'Out there a couple of days ago.' Sir Lancelot sat at the small table covered with a green baize cloth, on which were set some folders, a pewter inkwell with a steel-nibbed pen, a brass clock, a small pewter bowl with one odd, squared-off side, a bell to be struck by the palm of the hand, as once summoned the landlord in sleepy country pubs, and several large bottles containing pickled human organs attacked with flamboyant if implicitly mystifying disease. 'Caught a ten-pound rainbow.'

'No!'

'Nothing to it, really,' Sir Lancelot continued modestly. 'I'd had my eye on him for some time. Rather tricky cast, admittedly, under a low bridge. Had to play him for almost an hour before popping him in the net. But no real trouble.'

'I must congratulate you, Lancelot. That must be the record weight, or damn near it.'

'It was quite a substantial fish.'

'You're having it stuffed, of course?'

'Unfortunately it has been eaten by cats.'

'Oh, no!'

'They belonged to my housekeeper. My former housekeeper.'

'But what a disaster.'

'The worst of its kind, I should say, since John Stuart Mill's parlourmaid lit the fire with the manuscript of Carlyle's *French Revolution*. But one must rise above it.' He hitched up his trouser-creases briskly. 'Now to work. I asked out-patients to send me up a fibroadenoma of the breast. That shouldn't strain the mentality of even the Bleeders candidates.'

'I always rather like examining for the Bleeders,' the other surgeon said fondly. 'So much more intimate than those awful massed battles between students and examiners for the university degree.'

'I suppose the Bleeders are a useful safety-net, for those who grasp somewhat weakly the trapezes swinging dizzily through the higher atmosphere of medicine,' Sir Lancelot observed philosophically. 'Though it isn't half so intimate as in the days when they held it in Bleeders Hall and provided free beer to refresh the flagging candidates.'

'I find they always make excellent doctors, when they finally *do* pass. And after all, the Worshipful Company established its right to examine apprentices only through bleeding our Monarchy for several centuries.'

'Yes, and nearly exsanguinating our nobility into the bargain.' Sir Lancelot picked up the lopsided pewter dish. 'Odd how these bleeding bowls turn up in antique shops. One sometimes sees them filled with violets in tasteful homes.'

The ward sister put her head round the screen. 'There's a young lady come up to see you, Sir Lancelot.'

'That'll be the fibroadenoma. Pop her behind a screen, sister, and tell her to take her things off. Say that I shall want to have a look at her breasts.'

'Very good, Sir Lancelot.'

'And send in the first candidate.'

A tall, fair, red-faced man with a large moustache, approaching middle age, in a tweed suit and with a jaunty air, took the chair opposite. 'Ah, Mr Pottle. Delighted to see you again. It is always pleasant with this examination, we and the students coming to know each other so well over the years. Tenth time, isn't it?'

'Twelfth, Sir Lancelot,'

'Very well, Mr Pottle. You are woken in the middle of the night. It's the police. They whisk you in their car to a luxurious flat in Mayfair. There you see a glamorous model lying on the carpet, starkers. You diagnose barbiturate poison. What treatment do you give?'

'Hot coffee and blankets, sir.'

'She's unconscious, you fool.'

'Hot coffee and blankets per rectum, sir.'

Sir Lancelot passed a hand over his eyes. 'Very well. What are the signs of phosphorus poisoning?'

'I say, "Luminous motions, sir," and you say, "A mere flash in the pan, my boy." We all know that hoary old one puts you in a good mood, sir. But if I may say so, I'm getting rather tired of it.'

Sir Lancelot grunted. 'Possibly you're right. Come and have a look at this patient over here. Yes, sister, what is it?' he added testily.

'It's that young woman, Sir Lancelot. She's refusing to take her bra off.'

'Really, some people are impossible these days. Always standing on their dignity. How does she expect me to help her if she doesn't let the dog see the rabbit? Tell her I've felt more tits than she's had hot dinners.'

'Very well, Sir Lancelot.'

Lying in his pyjamas on an examination couch behind another pair of screens was Mr Winterflood, the technician from the clinical pathology laboratory. 'Good morning, Sir Lancelot,' he began eagerly. 'Delighted to be of assistance again. By displaying my wares, as you might say.'

'Morning, Winterflood. And don't let me hear you flogging your diagnosis to the candidates.'

'Sir Lancelot! I'd never do a thing like that.'

'I heard you'd reduced the price from five quid to three quid-fifty. I'm very cheered. It shows the candidates must be getting cleverer.' He turned to the middle-aged student. 'Just take a look at this fellow, then come and tell me what you find. He's enjoying a day's holiday from the hospital staff, so he knows all the answers. By the way, I happen to know that you, Mr Pottle, and everyone else are aware that Winterflood is the one with the enlarged spleen. But he has lots of other things as well, and under local rules this morning spleens don't count.'

Sir Lancelot went back to the table and slapped his palm on the bell. A thin, delicate-looking young man in a stylish blue suit appeared. Sir Lancelot frowned. 'Take a seat, please. I don't fancy we've ever met, have we?'

'I can't recall as much, sir.'

'Name?'

'Chisley, sir.'

'And you are from?'

'I'm a London man, sir.'

'From the London, eh? What would you do if you came into my study one evening and found me howling on the hearth-rug with a pain in my belly?'

'I should send for a doctor, sir.'

Sir Lancelot glared. 'Don't give me any insolence, please.' He pushed across a cylindrical jar. 'What's that?'

'I'm afraid I haven't the vaguest idea, sir.'

'It's a tape worm.'

'Ugh!'

'You don't seem to have prepared yourself very well, Mr Chisley. I'm surprised at that, in a candidate from the London Hospital.'

'I'm not from any hospital, sir. I was sent by the domestic agency.'

A young, pretty blonde girl burst through the screens. 'Which one's Sir Lancelot Spratt?' she demanded furiously. 'You with the beard? I've a damn good mind to report you to the Ministry. And the police. I'm a *cordon bleu*, not a concubine.'

Sir Lancelot jumped up. Another pair of screens flew apart and the dean burst in, followed by Josephine. 'Lancelot – Winterflood. Where is he? We've been searching all the labs. Ah! He's behind there –'

'Dean! This is an examination, not a roughhouse –'

'Winterflood –' The dean elbowed the startled Mr Pottle aside. 'Last Monday, did you or did you not do a pregnancy test on a specimen of my daughter's urine?'

'I am not at liberty to discuss my patients –'

'Don't try that rubbish. Answer yes or no, or you're more redundant than a eunuch's jock-strap.'

'Lionel!' cried Josephine.

'Yes, sir. I did.'

'And was it or was it not positive?'

'Positive, sir.'

The dean banged his forehead with his fist. 'To think! That I credited my daughter with enough sense, as a St Swithin's student, to know if she was pregnant or not. And she based her diagnosis on one bloody urine test! She must be out of her head.'

'But it was certainly positive, sir,' said Winterflood defensively. 'I repeated it twice. In the young lady's very presence.'

'Well, she isn't pregnant. She was a few days late, that's all. As you might expect in a girl of somewhat tense disposition, like her mother.'

'Well, that should clear the air a bit,' put in Sir Lancelot over the dean's shoulder.

'Mr Winterflood,' asked Josephine calmly. 'Did you last Monday test another specimen? One that, for various reasons, it was thought best not to bring to the notice of the professor?'

Winterflood looked from one to the other. 'I did.'

'And was it positive or negative?'

'Negative.' He shifted anxiously on the couch. 'I thought that reasonable, in view of the patient's...well, age.'

'And I agree, Mr Winterflood. I thought myself the symptoms were due to the onset of the menopause. But I'm afraid you did rather muddle the specimens up – even with the same name on the two labels.'

'What on earth is everyone talking about?' demanded the dean crossly.

'Oh, Lionel! We're going to have another little one.'

'Cor,' muttered the dean.

'It all fits in,' said Josephine radiantly. 'It was the night of the May ball – after your lovely champagne party, Lancelot.'

The dean wagged a finger. 'Lancelot! It's all your responsibility.'

'It isn't, old cock. But thanks for the flattery.'

'I feel faint,' said the dean.

'Sister! Bring a glass of water.'

'I'm so happy,' said Josephine, 'that I feel quite woozy myself.'

'Sister! Two glasses of water.'

'Here, what about my exam?' asked Mr Pottle.

'You've passed.'

'I might say, I did not come here to be shown tapeworms,' said the man from the agency. 'You're all dead kinky if you ask me.'

'I want my travelling expenses,' added the girl. 'Breasts, indeed!'

'George,' said Sir Lancelot calmly to the other examiner. 'Would you be a pal and sort all this out? I think I'm going fishing.'

25

Edgar Sharpewhistle was standing in the main hall of St Swithin's, talking to Tulip Twyson and looking gloomy.

'I can't go ahead with it.'

'But you *must*, Edgar.'

'It's impossible. I'm shattered. Confused and totally demoralized. If I got in the television studio now, I wouldn't have the IQ of a village idiot. I've been trying out my mind with a very simple test – just using the alphabet backwards and forwards alternately, to get the numbers to multiply and divide successively, you know. But I couldn't do it. I just couldn't. I'm going to withdraw and say I've got jaundice, or something. Let someone else win the thousand quid. It just isn't worth it.'

'Edgar, this is pure defeatism.'

'That's fair enough, then, isn't it? I've just been defeated. I thought I had a wife and family. Now I find I haven't either. Never did have, if it comes to that.'

She put her arm through his. 'But Edgar, you're not sorry, really?'

'Of course I am.'

She smoothed his tie. 'Your pride may be dented, but surely that's eminently repairable? Listen – you were going to marry Muriel because you thought she was having your baby. Right?'

'It was the correct thing to do, wasn't it?'

'Of course it was, Edgar dear. Very honourable. But if you knew then what you know now – that there was a slip-up in the lab, rather than in the bedroom – would you have been quite so enthusiastic?'

Sharpewhistle scratched his right ear. 'Nice girl, Muriel.'

'And the dean's daughter. But had she not been his daughter…and dear Muriel is just the teeniest, weeniest bit bossy, isn't she?'

'She's got a forceful personality, certainly. Might push a feller about.'

'My dear Edgar, *I* could tell you some things about Muriel and her forceful character.'

'Go on?'

'I know her intimately, don't forget.' Tulip started to walk him down the main corridor. 'I don't think a man of your brilliance would have liked scraping away on the second fiddle to *her*.'

'Well…perhaps not.'

'You're well out of it, if you ask me. Now you thank your lucky stars for the escape, and apply yourself to winning the *IQ Quiz*.'

He shook his head slowly. 'I just couldn't do it. In my present state, I'd be the laughing stock of the studio.'

'Think of the honour of St Swithin's.'

'Balls to the honour of St Swithin's.'

'Think of your fellow students.'

'Why should I? They've never been particularly nice to me, not all the time I've been here.'

'I think they have, Edgar – compared with how they'll behave if you scratch from *IQ Quiz*. You must at least make an effort. Just think of all that money they've put on you.' Sharpewhistle looked thoughtful. 'And just think of what we told you yesterday lunchtime in the common-room. Or would you really relish a Guinness enema? Some men are so peculiar these days.'

'Perhaps…perhaps I will have a try.'

'That's the spirit.'

'I tell you what. I'll withdraw from the exam for the hospital gold medal. That'll ease the strain. Muriel can win it. I hope she likes it,' he said sourly. 'But I shan't win the quiz show. Not in my present state of mind. I'm inconsolable.'

'I bet you're not.'

'I am. Inconsolable.'

'Do you think, Edgar, that *I* might console you?'

He stopped, looking at her blankly.

'I fancy you, Edgar, you know. It's nice to think of all that brain-power behind it. Besides, I'd just love to help you spend that thousand quid.'

'You mean, Tulip, you'd – '

'You can take me out tonight. The other two girls in my flat are away.' He nodded violently.

'But you've got to promise, Edgar – you're going to win that quiz.'

'Tulip, I can feel my IQ rising already.'

'By the way, Edgar love, have you thought of using a deodorant – ?'

They jumped aside, as Sir Lancelot bore down on them at a trot.

He hurried through the main hall, past the plate-glass doors, down the front steps and across the courtyard. He looked neither right nor left, ignoring greetings from staff and students. He had to find himself on the calm banks of the river as soon as possible, or he felt he would blow up. Life was becoming outrageously complicated at St Swithin's. Besides, there now seemed no prospect of anyone coming to look after him and cook his dinners, ever.

He opened the front door of No 3. He stopped. Something was different in the hall. The table had been out of place, the carpet rucked, there had been sheets of yesterday's papers over the floor. Now all was tidy, dusted and gleaming with furniture polish. A subdued tinkle came from the dining-room. He pushed open the door.

'I took the liberty of assuming you'd be lunching at home today, Sir Lancelot,' said Miss MacNish, wearing her usual cornflower blue overall. 'I thought you'd care for one of my cheese souffles to start with, followed by some grilled kidneys and tomato. And I've made an apple pie.'

'You've come back,' he exclaimed.

She looked surprised. 'Back? Oh, yes, Sir Lancelot, I *was* away for a couple of nights, I suppose. I'll repay you from my days off.'

He stood stroking his beard. 'I am of course delighted to see you...Fiona.'

'Thank you, Sir Lancelot. It's always agreeable to be appreciated.' She went on laying the table.

'Where are the cats?' he asked suddenly.

'The cats' home, Sir Lancelot. I felt they could be better looked after by professional keepers. They are very complicated cats.'

157

'I'm sure that was very wise of you. I expect that home could do with some cash? I'll send them a substantial donation, in fact, I might mention them in my will.'

'You are very kind and generous, as always, Sir Lancelot.'

'May I take it that you found your previous employment…or should I say, the company in which you spent your two days' holiday, not entirely congenial?'

'Dr Bonaccord and myself, sir, are not speaking. Neither is Mrs Tennant.'

'Yes, these psychiatrists are most unreliable and inconsiderate people. Wanted meals at irregular hours and screamed if the soup was cold, I shouldn't wonder?'

'That I should not object to, Sir Lancelot. It would be part of my employment. But what I will not stand is immorality.'

'But my dear Miss MacNish! Surely you went to No 1 with your eyes open? Everyone in St Swithin's knows Bonaccord's living with his secretary in the fullest and most enjoyable sense of the word.'

'I knew that, sir, of course. I can be broad-minded, sir, as broad as anyone. Though I must say, some of the things you see and hear these days make you wonder. But there are *some* things, sir, which I think are going too far. Too far altogether. Look, sir –' She felt in her overall pocket. 'I was dusting round her desk earlier this morning… I wasn't prying, or anything, sir, but she said it was always locked to keep inquisitive people out, so I tried it, just idly, sir, and it wasn't locked properly, it just opened in my hands like that. And what do you think I found inside? Just look at this photograph.'

Sir Lancelot took it. His hand trembled. 'Good God! This is the most outrageously indecent thing I've seen in my entire life.'

'I thought you'd say as much, sir.'

He tapped the photograph against his beard, filled with a sudden thought. 'Miss MacNish, you must admit that this sort of reprehensible antic must be stopped. It most certainly can't be allowed to continue in a respectable area like Lazar Row. Property owned by the hospital, too. I really feel it my duty, not only as a colleague of Bonaccord's at St Swithin's, but as an ordinary citizen, to take this up with him. He must be made to see the error of his ways.'

She looked doubtful. 'I shouldn't like him to know how you came to possess the photograph, sir.'

'Miss MacNish, I would only be doing my duty – an unpleasant duty, indeed a quite nauseating one – by confronting Bonaccord with this. I only ask you to accept it was your duty to collect this evidence and pass it to me.'

'Well… Aberdonians are not ones to flinch from doing their duty, sir.'

'Capital. I'm sure that's very noble of you. Bonaccord will, of course, by now have found it missing and realized anyway you'd walked off with it as a little keepsake. I think I'll call on him straight away. He usually works at home on Thursday mornings.'

'Would you care for tripe and onions for your dinner tonight, sir?'

'I was going fishing, but I shall stay specifically to eat them.'

'You are very kind, sir.' Miss MacNish set a fork carefully in place. 'It almost kills me, sir – the thought of your being looked after by another woman.'

Sir Lancelot strode briskly the few yards to No 1. Gisela Tennant opened the front door. 'Oh! I suppose you've come for Miss MacNish's things?'

'As far as I am aware, she has moved back lock, stock and barrel. I hope you found her satisfactory, in her somewhat brief tenure of office?'

'No. I didn't find her satisfactory at all. She was arrogant and insolent. And her taste in food was appalling. Jam roly-poly and tripe. Ugh!'

'I'm sorry she didn't suit. Is Dr Bonaccord in? I have another matter I am anxious to discuss with him.'

'He's busy writing a paper for *Psychological Medicine*.'

'Then I must interrupt him.'

She looked annoyed. 'Surely you could put it off till later?'

'I think not. By the way, Mrs Tennant, were you ever married?'

She stared at him, She bit her lip. 'Go on up.'

Sir Lancelot knocked on the door of the study and walked straight in. The psychiatrist looked up in irritation. 'If you are suffering another acute phobia about cats, Lancelot, I'm afraid you'll have to put up with it until this evening. I'm extremely busy. It's bad enough, suffering emotional scenes from your housekeeper – who, I might add, is a hysteric of quite severe degree… ' Sir Lancelot flourished the photograph, keeping a tight hold on it. 'You got that from Miss MacNish,' Dr Bonaccord said furiously.

'Exactly.'

'She stole it.'

'Well, you stole Miss MacNish in the first place.'

'I'll have her prosecuted.'

'You won't, you know.'

Dr Bonaccord fell silent. He stared again at the photograph in Sir Lancelot's fingers.

'Well?' asked Sir Lancelot.

Dr Bonaccord shrugged his shoulders. 'It is surely only our little aberrations in behaviour which make the human race at all interesting?'

'You think so, do you? I wonder what a criminal court would think?'

The psychiatrist looked alarmed. 'It wouldn't come to that, I hope? I mean, you wouldn't…or would you? Come, Lancelot! Don't be hard on us. After all, it's a harmless vice, if vice it is at all.'

'*I* think it's a vice, and so do all decent people, Bonaccord. I should say that even a good many people, whom I myself would *not* think of as decent, would shy away from your particular behaviour. Hippies, drug addicts and the like. They'd ostracize you. You are the lowest of the low.'

Dr Bonaccord looked at him imploringly. 'But if anything came out…it would be the end of my career… '

'I should imagine that would be among your minor troubles.'

'Lancelot…apart from this…this little failing surely you've always thought of me, and of Gisela, as perfectly upright, honest, well-integrated persons? Can't I appeal to your better nature? Don't you see how terrible it would be for her, not just for me, if this was blazoned in the public press?'

'The fact that you are a psychiatrist might make the public think it all perfectly excusable.'

'You're always making cheap jokes about psychiatrists.'

'I'm sorry if they upset you. Well, I'll bid you good morning, Bonaccord.' He pocketed the photograph. 'I can get a taxi to Scotland Yard.'

'Lancelot –'

He turned at the door. 'Yes?'

'I'm deeply sorry. And ashamed. Honestly, I am.'

'This is a rather sudden rush of contrition to the heart, isn't it?'

'It's you, Lancelot, You're such an upright, honest, completely *straight* man, it shames me.'

He grunted. 'I don't believe you, Bonaccord, but I'm prepared to be merciful. I'll keep my mouth shut.'

'I knew a man of your own inner kindness –'

'On one condition.'

'My position is such that I can only ask you to name it.'

Sir Lancelot perched on the edge of the desk. 'A few days ago, Dr Frances Humble, MP, offered you the post of vice-chancellor of Hampton Wick University.'

Dr Bonaccord nodded nervously. 'That is correct.'

'You turned it down.'

'That, too, is correct.'

'Have you a pen, or a ballpoint? Good. Take one of those sheets of writing paper. I wish you to write to Dr Humble at the House of Commons.'

'But what have I got to say?'

'I can save you the trouble of composition "Dear Dr Humble – " Go on.' The psychiatrist started to write. ' "I must have been mad to refuse the Hampton Wick job. I accept it with enthusiasm – " '

'Lancelot! I can't.'

'You can.'

He hesitated. He wrote the letter. He signed it in silence.

'Thank you, Bonaccord. I shall address the envelope and deliver it by hand myself. I'm sure you'll be very happy at Hampton Wick. It will be very stimulating, to have so many young, active minds round you all the time. And doubtless your...your secretary will prove a charming hostess during those dreary old sit-ins the students keep conducting in the vice-chancellor's private quarters. Good morning.'

'Here – the photograph.'

'I shall keep this, if I may, until Monday morning, when the official announcement will be made about Hampton Wick. I should not like to expose you to the temptation of back-sliding. Then you shall have it back, on my word of honour. In a sealed envelope.'

Sir Lancelot opened the door. Gisela was standing immediately outside. He gave her a courtly bow. As the front door shut behind him, she went into the study.

'You heard, I suppose?' said the psychiatrist dully.

'Every word. Which photo was it?'

'Nothing special. Just one of you and I as kids with our mother and father. We needn't have kept it, really, except for sentimental reasons.'

'He knows we're brother and sister?'

'It wouldn't take a man like him long to latch on to *that*.'

'I suppose it'll be all round St Swithin's by tomorrow?'

'No, I don't think so. He'll keep his part of the bargain. He's a bastard, but a fair bastard.'

She sat on the edge of the easy chair. 'So we're to move?'

'I'd no alternative, had I? You don't blame me, Gissie, do you?'

'Of course not, Cedric. In a way it'll be a challenge for you.'

'It's a challenge, all right. I can only hope I'll be rather more successful than my predecessors.'

'I'm sure you'll be, Cedric. You're much cleverer,'

'At least we'll be together, won't we?'

'That's the important thing.'

'Perhaps we should kill off Mr Tennant? Make you a lovely young widow?'

'Perhaps we should. But I could hardly revert to my maiden name, could I?' She gave a wan smile. 'I'd better cut that old name-tape from my tennis shoe, before anyone else noses about.'

'At least *some* good's come out of all this. I managed to slip my scheme for these three houses through the hospital committee last night, entirely because the dean and Sir Lancelot were otherwise somewhat heavily engaged. It's an absolute disgrace, hospital property being used for the medical staff's living accommodation, when there's such a shortage of psychiatric beds. As the leases fall vacant, the houses will be put to good use housing psychopathic youths from the East End. If we get on with our packing, they should start moving in here within a couple of weeks. Now will you get me my violin, Gissie? I really feel that I need a little Mozart.'

26

'Lancelot!'

Sir Lancelot had just stepped out of No 1 into the bright midday sunshine. He turned to see the dean skipping hatless round the corner. 'I say, dean, are you all right now?'

'Splendid. Wonderful. Never been better. I'm having a baby.'

'So I gathered. Congratulations.'

'Come inside. I've got some champagne in the fridge.'

They went into No 2. The dean at last pulled the champagne cork and he poured the wine into a pair of glasses in his sitting-room.

'How's Josephine?' asked Sir Lancelot.

'Having a little lie-down at St Swithin's. Got to take life very carefully, you know. Though I'm sure everything's going to be all right. After all, she's still quite young, compared with me.' The dean gave a laugh. 'Looking back now, I must have been blind and deaf these last four days. Josephine took her specimen bottle to that rather awful fellow Winterflood early on Monday morning, with the excuse that she had to visit the physiotherapy department at St Swithin's about her back. She almost dropped dead when she ran into Muriel in the corridor immediately afterwards – I suppose poor Muriel didn't suspect anything, because she had enough on her own mind at the time. Then in the evening Josephine went to collect the result, telling me she'd gone to post a letter in the box outside St Swithin's. The duplicity of women!' he said gaily.

'No wonder Mata Hari got away with it for so long.'

'But why didn't Josephine just tell you she suspected she was in pod?'

'She thought I might say she was being stupid, unless she could produce firm evidence. I can't understand what put that idea in her head. Though of course, I should have made the diagnosis myself. She suddenly developed longings – for asparagus and plovers' eggs, of all things. The next day she had morning sickness, but I put it down to gastritis. And she had a peculiar emotional outburst about Frankie Humble. Still, I never was very brilliant at midwifery. To tell the truth, I thought it rather too messy, and the hours were terrible.'

'I hope it'll be another boy.'

'So do I.' The dean raised his glass. 'It all happened on *your* champagne, Lancelot. Well, well. Fancy that doing the trick. What brand was it? It might do to get in a case or two.'

'So you're pleased?'

'Delighted. In fact, it's saved my life. Absolutely saved it. I don't know if you noticed, but recently a certain melancholy has been coming over me…a certain sense of futility, of uselessness…of all my dreams and ambitions being fulfilled, and of it all perhaps hardly having been worth the trouble.'

'That the world was your oyster, but it had turned out a bad one?'

'Precisely. I had unpleasant physical symptoms, too. Fear of approaching dissolution. Not uncommon in men of our age, I'm sure? But now they've all gone. Flown! I have something to look forward to in life, someone to replace my other two children, who have gone off into the world. It's really most thrilling.'

'Could be twins, of course.'

'Good God, I never thought of that.' The dean swallowed his champagne quickly. 'I actually consulted Bonaccord about my mental state, you know. I don't think he really understood my case.'

'He's leaving Lazar Row.'

'Really? He said nothing to me.'

'And St Swithin's. He's taking another post. Vice-chancellor of Hampton Wick University.'

'Lancelot! How did you manage –'

'I have my methods, dean.'

'How splendid! I shan't be sorry to lose him as a neighbour. Though I must admit, his secretary decorates the street a bit. I wonder who'll move in?'

'It's a matter of indifference to me.'

'We want someone congenial, surely?'

'I shall be moving out.'

'Oh, come...'

'My dear dean, I suffered an intense phobia of Miss MacNish's cats. Bonaccord cured it overnight by making me pretend to myself they were little gurgling babies. I assure you that if I saw a baby now I should shake like an aspen and run like a hare. It is what, I believe, the psychiatric fraternity call "transference".'

'Perhaps you'll find somewhere comfortable near your fishing?' suggested the dean heartily. The notion of getting shot of Sir Lancelot as well as Bonaccord had a certain appeal. It would be pleasant to rid himself of the onions. 'I shall stay on, of course. I have nowhere else I could possibly go. Muriel's flat will become our nursery suite, once she's married. I wonder who the hospital will put in your house? Doubtless they have plans for someone already.' He finished his drink. 'I'll be sorry to lose your company, I must say, Lancelot. I mean that most sincerely.'

'And I yours.'

'At least it isn't a permanent loss.'

'What do you mean?'

'Well...you're not dying, or anything like that.'

Sir Lancelot eyed him narrowly. 'Why should you say that?'

The dean looked uncomfortable. 'May I say something, Lancelot, which you may find as embarrassing to hear as I to utter? Quite frankly – and I did not seek the task, not for one moment, it was thrust on me and I had to do my duty – I have been entrusted with the exercise – the onerous, I might say painful, exercise – of preparing your obituary notice.'

'Don't get so worried about it, cock. I'm doing yours.'

The dean's mouth opened. 'When were you asked?'

'Monday morning.'

'But so was I.'

'Both been working hard, then, haven't we?'

'I found it incredibly difficult. I mean, to do you justice, Lancelot.'

'I'm sure you did,'

'Listen, Lancelot – it's a horrible task, almost like performing a post-mortem on you – '

'Thank you.'

'Surely you must find it equally distasteful? Why don't we both write our own? We can swap them, get them typed out, send them off to the editor, and no one will be any the wiser.'

'I say, dean, what a capital idea. Quite the best you've had for some time.'

'It's a great relief, Particularly as I've got so many happy thoughts in my mind. Well, I must get back to Josephine at the hospital. She deserves all the care and attention I can possibly foster on her.'

They parted. Sir Lancelot opened the front door of his own house. He staggered backwards as a Great Dane leapt up, put its paws on his shoulders and started licking his face.

'Oh, sir,' said Miss MacNish fondly from inside the hall. 'He likes you.'

Sir Lancelot struggled with his handkerchief. 'Miss MacNish…quite so…as it happens, I am very fond of dogs.'

'I'm sorry he's so playful, sir. But he's still only a puppy.'

'Good God,' muttered Sir Lancelot.

He shook off the animal. He mounted the stairs to his study. He drew towards him a blank pad of foolscap. He uncapped his fountain-pen. He wrote,

The tragic death yesterday of Sir Lancelot Spratt FRCS deprives the world of one of its greatest trout fishermen. He became a legend in his lifetime. There is a little-known story that he once landed a record rainbow trout of not less than fifteen pounds, to be deprived of it before its weight could be authenticated by a cruel accident…

At least, Sir Lancelot had a serene sense of values.

RICHARD GORDON

DOCTOR IN THE HOUSE

Richard Gordon's acceptance into St Swithin's medical school came as no surprise to anyone, least of all him – after all, he had been to public school, played first XV rugby, and his father was, let's face it, 'a St Swithin's man'. Surely he was set for life. It was rather a shock then to discover that, once there, he would actually have to work, and quite hard. Fortunately for Richard Gordon, life proved not to be all dissection and textbooks after all… This hilarious hospital comedy is perfect reading for anyone who's ever wondered exactly what medical students get up to in their training. Just don't read it on your way to the doctor's!

'Uproarious, extremely iconoclastic' – *Evening News*
'A delightful book' – *Sunday Times*

DOCTOR AT SEA

Richard Gordon's life was moving rapidly towards middle-aged lethargy – or so he felt. Employed as an assistant in general practice – the medical equivalent of a poor curate – and having been 'persuaded' that marriage is as much an obligation for a young doctor as celibacy for a priest, Richard sees the rest of his life stretching before him. Losing his nerve, and desperately in need of an antidote, he instead signs on with the Fathom Steamboat Company. What follows is a hilarious tale of nautical diseases and assorted misadventures at sea. Yet he also becomes embroiled in a mystery – what is in the Captain's stomach remedy? And more to the point, what on earth happened to the previous doctor?

'Sheer unadulterated fun' – *Star*

RICHARD GORDON

DOCTOR AT LARGE

Dr Richard Gordon's first job after qualifying takes him to St Swithin's where he is enrolled as Junior Casualty House Surgeon. However, some rather unfortunate incidents with Mr Justice Hopwood, as well as one of his patients inexplicably coughing up nuts and bolts, mean that promotion passes him by – and goes instead to Bingham, his odious rival. After a series of disastrous interviews, Gordon cuts his losses and visits a medical employment agency. To his disappointment, all the best jobs have already been snapped up, but he could always turn to general practice...

DOCTOR GORDON'S CASEBOOK

'Well, I see no reason why anyone should expect a doctor to be on call seven days a week, twenty-four hours a day. Considering the sort of risky life your average GP leads, it's not only inhuman but simple-minded to think that a doctor could stay sober that long...'

As Dr Richard Gordon joins the ranks of such world-famous diarists as Samuel Pepys and Fanny Burney, his most intimate thoughts and confessions reveal the life of a GP to be not quite as we might expect... Hilarious, riotous and just a bit too truthful, this is Richard Gordon at his best.

RICHARD GORDON

GREAT MEDICAL DISASTERS

Man's activities have been tainted by disaster ever since the serpent first approached Eve in the garden. And the world of medicine is no exception. In this outrageous and strangely informative book, Richard Gordon explores some of history's more bizarre medical disasters. He creates a catalogue of mishaps including anthrax bombs on Gruinard Island, destroying mosquitoes in Panama, and Mary the cook who, in 1904, inadvertently spread Typhoid across New York State. As the Bible so rightly says, 'He that sinneth before his maker, let him fall into the hands of the physician.'

THE PRIVATE LIFE OF JACK THE RIPPER

In this remarkably shrewd and witty novel, Victorian London is brought to life with a compelling authority. Richard Gordon wonderfully conveys the boisterous, often lusty panorama of life for the very poor – hard, menial work; violence; prostitution; disease. *The Private Life of Jack The Ripper* is a masterly evocation of the practice of medicine in 1888 – the year of Jack the Ripper. It is also a dark and disturbing medical mystery. Why were his victims so silent? And why was there so little blood?

'…horribly entertaining…excitement and suspense buttressed with
authentic period atmosphere' – *The Daily Telegraph*

TITLES BY RICHARD GORDON AVAILABLE DIRECT
FROM HOUSE OF STRATUS

Quantity	£	$(US)	$(CAN)	€
THE CAPTAIN'S TABLE	6.99	11.50	15.99	11.50
DOCTOR AND SON	6.99	11.50	15.99	11.50
DOCTOR AT LARGE	6.99	11.50	15.99	11.50
DOCTOR AT SEA	6.99	11.50	15.99	11.50
DOCTOR IN CLOVER	6.99	11.50	15.99	11.50
DOCTOR IN LOVE	6.99	11.50	15.99	11.50
DOCTOR IN THE HOUSE	6.99	11.50	15.99	11.50
DOCTOR IN THE NEST	6.99	11.50	15.99	11.50
DOCTOR IN THE NUDE	6.99	11.50	15.99	11.50
DOCTOR IN THE SOUP	6.99	11.50	15.99	11.50
DOCTOR IN THE SWIM	6.99	11.50	15.99	11.50
DOCTOR ON THE BALL	6.99	11.50	15.99	11.50
DOCTOR ON THE BOIL	6.99	11.50	15.99	11.50
DOCTOR ON THE JOB	6.99	11.50	15.99	11.50
DOCTOR ON TOAST	6.99	11.50	15.99	11.50
DOCTOR'S DAUGHTERS	6.99	11.50	15.99	11.50
DR GORDON'S CASEBOOK	6.99	11.50	15.99	11.50
THE FACEMAKER	6.99	11.50	15.99	11.50
GOOD NEIGHBOURS	6.99	11.50	15.99	11.50

ALL HOUSE OF STRATUS BOOKS ARE AVAILABLE FROM GOOD BOOKSHOPS OR
DIRECT FROM THE PUBLISHER:

Internet: **www.houseofstratus.com** including author interviews, reviews, features.

Email: **sales@houseofstratus.com** please quote author, title and credit card details.

TITLES BY RICHARD GORDON AVAILABLE DIRECT
FROM HOUSE OF STRATUS

Quantity		£	$(US)	$(CAN)	€
	GREAT MEDICAL DISASTERS	6.99	11.50	15.99	11.50
	GREAT MEDICAL MYSTERIES	6.99	11.50	15.99	11.50
	HAPPY FAMILIES	6.99	11.50	15.99	11.50
	INVISIBLE VICTORY	6.99	11.50	15.99	11.50
	LOVE AND SIR LANCELOT	6.99	11.50	15.99	11.50
	NUTS IN MAY	6.99	11.50	15.99	11.50
	THE SUMMER OF SIR LANCELOT	6.99	11.50	15.99	11.50
	SURGEON AT ARMS	6.99	11.50	15.99	11.50
	THE PRIVATE LIFE OF DR CRIPPEN	6.99	11.50	15.99	11.50
	THE PRIVATE LIFE OF FLORENCE NIGHTINGALE	6.99	11.50	15.99	11.50
	THE PRIVATE LIFE OF JACK THE RIPPER	6.99	11.50	15.99	11.50

ALL HOUSE OF STRATUS BOOKS ARE AVAILABLE FROM GOOD BOOKSHOPS OR
DIRECT FROM THE PUBLISHER:

Hotline: UK ONLY: 0800 169 1780, please quote author, title and credit card details.
INTERNATIONAL: +44 (0) 20 7494 6400, please quote author, title and
credit card details.

Send to: House of Stratus Sales Department
24c Old Burlington Street
London
W1X 1RL
UK

S-WES/3480/09/2

Please allow for postage costs charged per order plus an amount per book as set out in the tables below:

	£(Sterling)	$(US)	$(CAN)	€(Euros)
Cost per order				
UK	2.00	3.00	4.50	3.30
Europe	3.00	4.50	6.75	5.00
North America	3.00	4.50	6.75	5.00
Rest of World	3.00	4.50	6.75	5.00
Additional cost per book				
UK	0.50	0.75	1.15	0.85
Europe	1.00	1.50	2.30	1.70
North America	2.00	3.00	4.60	3.40
Rest of World	2.50	3.75	5.75	4.25

PLEASE SEND CHEQUE, POSTAL ORDER (STERLING ONLY), EUROCHEQUE, OR INTERNATIONAL MONEY ORDER (PLEASE CIRCLE METHOD OF PAYMENT YOU WISH TO USE)
MAKE PAYABLE TO: STRATUS HOLDINGS plc

Cost of book(s): ——————— Example: 3 x books at £6.99 each: £20.97

Cost of order: ——————— Example: £2.00 (Delivery to UK address)

Additional cost per book: ——————— Example: 3 x £0.50: £1.50

Order total including postage: ——————— Example: £24.47

Please tick currency you wish to use and add total amount of order:

☐ £ (Sterling)   ☐ $ (US)   ☐ $ (CAN)   ☐ € (EUROS)

VISA, MASTERCARD, SWITCH, AMEX, SOLO, JCB:

☐☐☐☐☐☐☐☐☐☐☐☐☐☐☐☐☐☐☐

Issue number (Switch only):

☐☐☐

Start Date: **Expiry Date:**

☐☐/☐☐   ☐☐/☐☐

Signature: ——————————————

NAME: ————————————————————————

ADDRESS: ————————————————————————

————————————————————————

POSTCODE: ——————

Please allow 28 days for delivery.

Prices subject to change without notice.
Please tick box if you do not wish to receive any additional information. ☐

House of Stratus publishes many other titles in this genre; please check our website (**www.houseofstratus.com**) for more details.